Times Like These

Published by Jan Stryvant

#64482

ISBN: 9781688538368

Jan Stryvant Books:

Distractions

Sean looked at the fort through his binoculars. "Well, at least it took them a month," he said with a sigh.

"Still," Chad said with a grumble, "if we hadn't shot the barrels out of all our artillery pieces, we *might* have held them off a few more weeks!"

Sean shook his head and snorted. "I doubt it. Sooner or later, they were going to start pushing their mages and stuff through the gateway and start erecting magical barriers."

Sean watched as a shell came in and exploded against the barrier that was now a hundred feet above the fort. All it was now was an annoyance to the djevels working on the fort, if that.

"Why are you still shelling them, anyway?"

"Just to let them know we're still here. Also, if for any reason it falls or they drop it, we'll know immediately and take advantage of it. My magic user consultants tell me the shield does take damage, so if they don't keep repairing it, eventually it'll be destroyed."

Sean nodded and looked a bit closer at the construction.

"I wonder if they're going to try and enclose the gateway?"

Chad shrugged. "I don't see what the point of that would be. Do we know for sure just how big it will get?"

"About a hundred yards from side to side."

"Well then, won't they have to build a ramp up to the middle to get full use of it?"

Sean thought about that. If it was him, he'd build four or five ramps, all at different levels, to get the best movement through the gateway.

"You know what?" Sean said, pulling the binoculars away from his face and looking over at Chad. "I have no idea. Yeah, I'd think they'd be doing something, but so far they're not. I'd guess they do on the other side, because the djevels coming out of it seem to be coming out of the middle."

"Maybe it's because they don't plan on sending anyone back?" Max suggested.

Sean looked at Chad, who shrugged.

"They're not the brightest or the most imaginative," Estrella offered. "Remember, they didn't actually build the gateways or the hellige points. They just took them over after they moved in and figured out how they worked."

"How long do you think until they start pushing out of there?" Sean asked, changing the subject.

Chad lead them back towards their waiting helicopter. "At the rate they're pouring out of there, I'm guessing as soon as the sun sets tonight."

"Why then?"

Chad shrugged. "Because that's when they've always tried to push out in the past?"

"And nothing came out of the small gateway last night, right?"

"Nothing. I'm thinking now that their fort at the main gateway is secure, they don't want to waste any more time with those. They just want to concentrate their efforts here."

"Not the brightest idea if you ask me." Sean chuckled.

"I'll take what I can get. Are you still set on launching an expedition through one?"

"You're just mad because you can't come," Estrella replied.

"Damn straight," Chad replied with a sour look on his face. "That's where the real fight is, after all."

"Yeah, yeah," Sean sighed, "down boy..." Sean stopped then and looked around; something was going on, something magical.

"You feel that?" Sean asked.

"What?" the others asked, all looking at him.

There was an explosion of magic then, and what Sean could only describe as hundreds of magical missiles came flying over the hill, tagging people and equipment everywhere. The helicopter was hit just below the main rotor, blowing off panels, throwing shrapnel up into the main rotor, and causing the whole thing to spin around and fall on its side, shedding blades and parts everywhere.

Any piece of equipment larger than a suitcase was also hit, which destroyed all their unarmored vehicles, and a good deal of their larger electronic equipment. People were dropping everywhere, stunned or wounded by the missiles that hit them. Sean's shield sucked it up, but he found himself doling out healing spells to Estrella, Cali, Max, and Chad immediately to keep them from being stunned.

Turning around, Sean ran back up to the top of the hill to see what was going on as the sound of a thousand voices roaring came from the gateway.

Dropping prone as he reached the top, he could see there was now a large demon of a type he hadn't seen before standing at the front of the fort as the gates of the fort opened. Hundreds of gnashers and bonde with råge driving them were pouring out of the gates, along with the occasional ridder or biskop in the group.

"What the hell is that?" he muttered

"That's a demon lord," Estrella muttered back. "A fairly powerful one, too, possibly one of Prince Talt's if I don't miss my guess."

"You know him then?"

Estrella shook her head. "No, but the badge he's wearing on that chain around his neck looks like one of Talt's."

Sean looked around at the defenders. A lot of them were down, thought he wasn't sure many, if any, of them were dead. That missile was a hell of a jolt, but he got the feeling it was more of a diversion than an actual attempt to kill everyone, and the way they were pouring out of the gates unchallenged showed it was working.

"How many of those do you think he can throw?" Sean asked as he pulled his rifle around and started firing on the lord.

"If he could do another one of those, he'd already have done it," Estrella said with a grunt as she started firing with her own rifle.

Sean noticed that the lord had cast a shield on himself.

"Well, he's obviously not tapped out yet," Sean said as he played the magic missile he'd gotten hit with back out of his buffer and targeted it at the lord. Interestingly enough, it penetrated the shield and caused the demon lord to turn and look right at where Sean was.

"Uh-oh, I think he sees us!" Estrella said.

"Good!" Sean growled and, leaping to his feet, he waved his rifle, then hosed down the area around the demon lord.

"What?" Sean yelled down at the lord. "Did I *hurt* you?" Sean flicked out another missile. They weren't very powerful, but apparently they were annoying. He'd have to examine the spell when he got the time later tonight.

"You will die, Lion!" the demon lord screeched and threw several more of those missile things at Sean, which his shield just absorbed and fed him the power behind them.

"Oh? And just who's going to kill me? You? I don't think so, you low-level bonde-humping toad! Why don't you go get your daddy, Prince Talt? Or is he too much of coward to even show his face?"

"What are you doing!" Estrella hissed from the ground.

"Trying to get pig face to come up here where I can kill him," Sean whispered back.

"He's a demon lord! And he's got an army!"

"Well, I got one of those, too. Speaking of which," Sean looked over at Chad who was giving orders to a group of werewolves, each one sprinting off as soon as he moved to the next, "I thought you said 'tonight'?"

"Tonight, this afternoon, what's a few hours between friends?" Chad grumbled and went back to telling his messengers what to do.

Sean looked back at the demon lord who was still screeching at him.

"Hey!" Sean yelled and cast a flame strike down at him. The shield parted the strike, but the ridder that had moved up to stand beside the lord was suddenly immolated, along with a couple dozen bonde and their råge leader. "You just gonna sit down there and scream insults like a gnasher? Or are you gonna come up here and play?"

Sean looked down at Estrella, "What's a good insult to a demon lord?"

"What? Are you crazy?"

"After all this time, you have to ask?" Cali grumbled. "Just tell him."

"Challenge him. If he refuses, he will lose face in front of everyone."

"Hey! Pigface! I challenge you!" Sean yelled.

"You can't challenge me!" the demon lord screeched back.

"Oh! You're scared! I get it! Well, that's okay. Maybe someone else then?"

Sean was amazed at the transformation in the demon lord's attitude as it drew out its sword and charged up the hill.

"Well, that hit the mark, Husband," Cali said with a laugh.

"Talt doesn't like lords who are cowards," Estrella said, enlightening them. "With a jibe like that, if he doesn't fight now, he won't live long."

"Great!" Sean said and tossed his rifle to Estrella as he drew his own sword. "Once I got him tied up, shoot him in the back."

"That's a violation of the rules!" Estrella exclaimed.

Sean grinned. "I know. Which is why I'm doing it. I cheat, remember?"

Turning back to the charging demon lord, Sean watched as he came up the hill. Sean quickly checked his mana levels—all the multipliers helped with any casting he wanted to do, but his healing abilities didn't get that benefit, and of course took directly from his pool. He had a feeling he was probably going to need those abilities, so looking back at the lord, he cast one more flame strike, setting the bonde and the råge that were charging up behind him on fire. Cali, Estrella, Maxine, and the members of his security detail and the other soldiers who were no longer stunned were all shooting at the djevels following the lord up the hill.

Chad was still busy passing orders, but he had a pistol in his hand, and every once in a while he would look up and shoot something, usually in the head.

They clashed then, Sean and the demon lord. Sean was surprised that the lord tried to bowl him over, bulling into him. Sean parried the lord's initial thrust, then dropped his right shoulder and took the demon right in the chest, knocking him back.

The lord was a foot taller than Sean, standing about nine-foot-tall, putting his throat right by Sean's muzzle, which he opened and, lunging up, he snapped his jaws closed, just barely missing.

The demon lord was swearing at himself as he pushed back to gain fighting space, and Sean smiled, showing all his teeth. Of course Sean was berating himself as well; if he'd just been a little quicker, this fight would already be over.

"I will end you, Lion! Your skull will decorate my hall!"

"Yeah, how 'bout you come a little closer, pigface, and let me get a taste this time!" Sean growled back, then was quickly fighting for his life, as the lord didn't hesitate an instant and started in with his sword.

Sean growled again, but this time he was concentrating completely on his sword work and not getting cut by the demon lord's blade. The lord was obviously a very accomplished swordsman, and Sean had to struggle just to keep up. He could see why Estrella had thought he was crazy for challenging him.

Sean also had the disadvantage of having to give ground as the forces around him were pushed back, lest he find himself surrounded by djevels and they do to him what he'd told Estrella to do.

But retreating as he fought did have its benefits. It put the demon lord higher than Sean as they first came down the hill, which allowed Sean to go for lower targets and limited the places he himself could be hit. True, his head was now that place, but it's easier to defend when the enemy's targets are limited.

Twice Sean darted in to attack the lord's legs with his free hand. The first time he got his claws in and drew that black ichor they called blood. The second time he wasn't so lucky and got kicked in the face for his trouble.

Sean popped a healing spell to deal with that and spent the next several minutes defending furiously. When it was done, they were on level ground, and from what he could see, Estrella and Cali were fighting furiously with their swords to either side of him, with more soldiers fanning out along the line to either side using either swords or rifles with bayonets.

And still the fight went on. As they started to retreat up the rise behind them, Sean's head came level with the demon lord's, and with a flick of his hand, he cast one of those magic missiles, planted himself and lunged forward, scoring a hit on the lord, his first major one in this fight.

Which caused the lord to redouble his efforts in a furious show of skill that almost cost Sean his head, and did earn him several cuts along his chest that were deep enough he had to pop another healing spell on himself or risk being caught out.

Sean waited a while as they continued to fight, and then made the same hand gesture he'd used the previous times to cast that magic missile, but as the demon lord flinched, he immediately followed up with an actual spell, another lower-powered flame jet, that he played all around the lord, once again setting many of the djevel fighters to either side on fire.

Sean then took two steps backwards. The lord immediately pursued, then stopped as he realized his mistake, and both Cali and Estrella struck him on the sides with their swords. As the lord tried to engage Estrella, Sean bulled forward and, striking the lord's blade to the side again, he dropped his shoulder and slammed into him again.

Snapping forward with his jaws, this time he got them on the demon lord's neck, if just barely, and was able to hold on for several seconds while being struck with the pommel on the lord's sword as he tried to free himself from Sean's jaws.

When he finally did free himself, Sean could see the lord was bleeding heavily from his neck as his line once again caught up with him, and Estrella and Cali had to go back to fighting to keep Sean from being encircled.

Looking up into the demon lord's eyes, Sean smiled and licked his lips.

"I'm *hungry*. Come to me, *food*!" Sean laughed and launched himself at the demon lord a second time, seeing a flicker of fear in the lord's eyes. He knew Sean could end him, and suddenly he started to fear that Sean was going to do just that. He hesitated just long enough that Sean was able to get through his guard and score a vicious blow, crippling one of the demon's arms, forcing him to switch over to a single-handed grip on his sword.

"Coward!" Sean roared as the line continued to move forward, almost carrying Sean away from the lord.

But then a most curious thing happened. The entire line to either side of the demon lord *stopped*. Noticing this, the lord's eyes widened, and Sean attacked immediately. Gone were the demon lord's well-practiced and skillful attacks; suddenly the lord's defense began to fall apart. His swordplay slowed, and his attacks stopped completely as he struggled to defend himself from Sean's attacks.

Sean saw it when it happened; the lord made a mistake, and his eyes went wide as he realized it. Sean leapt forward and, tossing his sword behind him, he shifted into his lion form. The last thing the lord saw was those huge, open jaws coming right for his head. Closing his jaws, Sean took the demon lord by the head and immediately began to whip his head from side to side, wringing the demon's neck and tossing his body back and forth.

The moment the lord died, Sean felt it. It wasn't just that his body had gone slack, but suddenly there was a welling up of energy inside him as he absorbed everything the demon lord *was*. Sean didn't know how to describe it; it was just an incredible rush of power, energy, and even some information. In that one moment, he knew everything there was to know about the lord he'd just killed, then it quickly started to fade away. Grabbing onto what the lord had known about magic, Sean tried to hold on to it, looking at it, thinking about it, trying to understand it before it was all gone.

But he didn't have time to tarry here now.

Turning from the fight, Sean dragged the lord up the rise behind him, almost prancing from the temporary energy rush, and then, in front of the entire djevel army, he sat down and began to eat.

The effect on the demon army was pronounced, but perhaps not as pronounced as Sean had hoped. They didn't retreat, but they stopped advancing, and started to dig in. As he watched, Sean saw his own troops disengage and start to retreat, carefully, pulling back and reorganizing. Looking up over the hills they had battled over, there were a lot more dead lycans than Sean would have liked.

Once his army had retreated out of sight of the enemy, Sean stood up, pissed on the carcass of the demon, and padded out of sight. Whereupon he stopped and puked his guts out for several minutes. He was still throwing up when Cali and Estrella found him.

"You had to eat him, didn't you?" Estrella said shaking her head.

"What's wrong with eating them?" Cali asked.

"Other than the taste?" Sean replied between retches. "I think I burned a half-dozen heals on my stomach alone."

"Then why did you do it, Husband?" Cali asked.

"Because it scared them," Estrella said, answering her. "Not enough to get them to retreat, they're still plenty afraid of their own commanders. Though I daresay once they learn that old Holigart there won't be coming back, they'll fear lions a whole lot more than they already do."

Sean nodded and got to his paws a little shakily. "Let's get out of here; I need to eat a cow to get the taste of that thing out of my muzzle." Sean looked around. "Did anyone grab my sword?"

"Travis did, I have it now," Cali said.

As they walked off with Sean stumbling between them, Estrella sighed. "You know, if you shifted back, I could just carry you."

"Can't, too tired," Sean grumbled.

"I told you not to do it, didn't I?"

"And you say the princes are worse than that?"

"Way worse."

Sean sighed and shook his head. "We need better weapons."

"Yes, we do."

"Where's Chad?"

"He pulled back to the command center to oversee the disposition of the troops."

"Does that mean we're not encircling them anymore?"

Estrella shook her head. "I don't know, you'll have to ask him."

By then they'd caught up with the troops, who appeared to be digging in, but where they'd been setting up in an encircling line in the past, it now looked like they were setting up fire control bases. He'd have to ask Chad about it.

"Can we get a helicopter back to the ranch?" Sean asked the first officer he came across.

"Not yet, they're still putting spells on them to protect them from magical attacks. But I've already called for ground transport, Sean."

Sean nodded and sat down on his butt. "I need to talk to Chad, but I lost my radio during the fight."

"Well, I'd offer mine," the officer said, "but I don't think it'd fit on your head."

Sean snorted and stretched out. "Anybody got anything to eat? I still got this horrid taste in my mouth."

"I'll see what I can find," he said and quickly walked off.

Twenty minutes later they were riding in the back of a noisy, but well-armored vehicle as Sean finished eating a large pork shoulder they'd found for him. Stretching out, he took stock of his condition. His mana levels were low, but they were regenerating now that he'd had a bite to eat and was resting. Shifting back to his hybrid form, he cast a silence spell on the vehicle and moved to one of the seats.

"I did that!" he called out as the driver was suddenly looking around, a bit shocked.

"Oh! Thank you, Sir!"

Sean just shook his head. "How long until we make it back to the ranch?"

"About an hour, Sir."

"Great. Get on the radio and arrange for someone to pick us up somewhere up ahead."

"I think the helicopters are still down, Sir."

"Yeah, I'm sure, tell them I'm not asking, I'm ordering."

"Ahhh..." The driver hesitated a moment, but obviously realized quickly that this wasn't his argument. "I'll tell them, Sir."

"Thanks."

Sean sat down, and with nothing better to do, he looked at the magic missile spell that was still sitting in his buffer. As spells went, it was a pretty simple little thing, but as he waded into it, he found its simplicity to be deceptive. If you just flung them out there without a target, they'd be drawn to anything over a certain size, living or otherwise.

It took him a while to figure out that the ones that had been draw to the helicopter and equipment weren't targeted at all; in fact, he'd bet they'd all been intended for people and not machines or equipment. But the electrical current in the devices fooled them into thinking they were living beings and drew them in like a magnet.

That gave him a few ideas for ways to protect against such attacks in the future.

The next thing he figured out about the spell was just how disruptive it was, for was all that it was weakly powered. Against living beings, it only did a little damage, but the effect it had on the body's nervous system was a lot like that of a taser. Sean could understand why that damaged electronic equipment, but he was at a loss as to why it had killed the helicopter.

Oh well, he'd tell Daelyn how it worked and leave it to her to figure out.

"Helicopter's here!" the driver called out, and Sean felt the vehicle stop.

"Thanks!" Sean said and followed the girls up out of the vehicle. Keeping their heads down, they ran over to the Black Hawk that was idling there for them. Jumping up in the back, Sean waved to Trey, the pilot.

"Happy to see you're still with us, Trey!" Sean shouted as the crew closed the doors and Trey lifted them off the ground.

"Happy to still be here!" Trey called back.

"Pass on that I expect all section heads and leaders to be in the conference room by the time we land!"

"You got it, Sean!"

Reaction

Prince Talt was 'dressing down' one of his subordinates, which in this case meant he had slaughtered the ridder that had displeased him, and was feasting on his life essence. The problem, Talt had always observed, was that once you became a prince, your requirements for food increased accordingly. Like everyone else, he was quite looking forward to setting foot out on the fruitful plains of this legendary jagtområder.

To be able to once again gorge himself as he had not done in far, far too long would be a wonderful feeling. He knew as a prince he would be able to journey to the jagtområder well before Sladd, his king, did. With the power he would quickly gain from the huge bounty of food there, he would easily be able to challenge Sladd and take the throne for himself.

He felt it then, a sudden weakening of his power! Jumping to his feet and drawing his sword, Prince Talt looked around his own throne room. Nothing was out of place, and his guards and servants were looking at him with obvious concern. Taking a moment, he took inventory of his vassals, going through them one by one, then he came across it... Lord Holigart was gone. Not just dead to reform in his hall when his soul had gathered back up to be reborn at his utsade, but gone, truly gone—his soul and his power consumed by another!

"Where was Lord Holigart's duty today?" Prince Talt demanded, turning to his personal scribe.

Penna quickly ran though his notes and answered.

"My Prince, he is at the main hellige point. His task is to lead his troops out of the fort and attack the cursed forces of the lions."

Prince Talt swore; this couldn't be the work of one of the other princes then, or even King Sladd.

"Huvudskydd," Prince Talt said, turning to one of his guardsmen. "Send a runner to the hellige. Find out what time Lord Holigart went through the portal and what happened to him!"

"At once, my Prince!" Huvudskydd said and dashed out of the room. One did not tarry when the Prince was angry, unless one wished to feed him as well.

Dropping back down into his throne, Prince Talt reviewed his options. Holigart was dead; there were no doubts as to that. He would need to raise up a new lord to take Holigart's place, one to bind Holigart's people to them so his power would not stay diminished. A great deal of Prince Talt's position came from the fifteen—now fourteen—lords that were bound to him. If he did not act quickly on this, one of the other five princes of King Sladd could send in their own man and steal Holigart's people away for themselves.

At least none of them would know he'd lost Holigart, as the lord had been in enemy territory.

"Penna, I need the names and status of all of Holigart's lieutenants."

"Yes, my Prince. Are you seeking to promote one?"

Prince Talt nodded.

Penna paged through his book until he came to the listing of Holigart's people.

"Well then, my Prince, allow me to begin," Penna said as he carefully read the list aloud.

Prince Talt was just finishing up the discussion with his scribe regarding who he would be favoring to take over for Holigart when a runner was escorted into his throne room by one of his guards.

"I bring news of Holigart, my Prince," the runner said, still panting heavily as he knelt before Prince Talt's throne.

"Speak," Prince Talt said with a gesture.

"Holigart was killed and eaten by a lion."

"I thought as much; how did it happen?"

"When Holigart first lead the charge, a lion appeared on a nearby hill and challenged him to personal combat while questioning Holigart's bravery and abilities. Holigart attacked, with his army supporting him. The lion used magic and fought Holigart for a quarter-daer, until the lion finally rose up, grabbed him by the head, dragged Holigart up on top of a hill were all could see him, and then he *ate* him."

"He drained his soul?"

"I do not know, my Prince. They said the lion ate lord Holigart, a piece at a time, tearing huge chucks out of him and swallowing them. As his troops watched."

Prince Talt sat back in his chair and blinked. He then turned to his scribe.

"Penna, has any lion ever *eaten* one of ours in this manner before?"

"Not that I know of, my Prince."

Prince Talt nodded. "Interesting." He then returned his attention to the runner. "What was the reaction of Holigart's forces?"

"They dug in, my Prince. Without him to lead them, they did not know what to do next. The report I was given said they did not stop out of fear, but because they did not know what to do."

"So they were too terrified to press forward, and too terrified to retreat," Penna whispered with a soft laugh.

Prince Talt tried not to laugh as well; his scribe Penna most likely had the right of it. Still, at least they did not retreat.

"Thank you, you may withdraw."

"Thank you, my Prince," the runner said and, getting up quickly, left the room.

"Huvudskydd," Prince Talt, said turning to his guard once more.

"Yes, my Prince?"

"Send a runner to the Hellige. Let them know that I am proud of them for not retreating. That I will assign a new leader to them shortly. Then send a second runner to lord Körsbär. Let him know he is now in charge of the attack."

"As you will it, my Prince!" Huvudskydd said and quickly left the room.

Dismissing the rest of his court, Prince Talt made his way back to his quarters. The small keep he was staying in was one he often used for those times during a pass when he needed to be nearby to oversee his people and his troops. Like most of the princes, he knew being too far away from the center of things could often end up with you no longer being a prince.

He did not bring more than one lord with him to these things, however. They were his powerbase after all, and risking more of them than he absolutely had to would be foolish. It would take several days for Körsbär to arrive and take leadership of Talt's forces.

This would mean that King Sladd would assign another prince to take over the fight for now. That did not sit well with Prince Talt. A great many of his plans had been prefaced with him being the first into the large feeding zone south of where the portal had opened in the jagtområder. Now he would have to refigure everything. Especially if he was going to take on Sladd before he had a chance to feed as well.

Ξ

Sean strode into the conference room with Cali and Estrella behind him. They'd taken the time to visit the armory, strip off their armor, and take a quick shower to get all the blood, gore, and dried pieces of dead djevel off.

Sean figured the extra time would give the others more time to assemble for this surprise meeting. Plus, he knew his armor was now in serious need of repair.

"Where do things stand, Chad?" Sean asked as he sat down. In front of his seat was a large pile of hamburgers on a tray. Grabbing one off the stack, he passed it to Cali, then another to Estrella, then one each to Roxy, Daelyn, Roberta, Jolene, and Peg, before sticking one in his own mouth. The first two he knew were almost as hungry as he was; the rest were more out of habit. He liked showing them his affection, and he made sure never to miss an opportunity, especially a public one like this.

"They've managed to push out anywhere from a half mile to a good mile from their fort by the gateway. That puts the line we have to defend at almost six miles long. The only thing that stopped their advance was the stunt you pulled with eating their leader."

Chad sighed and shook his head. "Stopped most of them in their tracks, and I can only guess, as the word went round, it stopped the rest of them, too."

"They're scared," Estrella volunteered between bites.

"Really?"

She nodded. "The king may rule, and the princes may be his might, but to the average demo..." Estrella glanced at Cali, who smiled, "...djevel, their lord is their everything. You have a connection with your lord because you work on their land, you work under their protection, you swear your allegiance directly to him. Not to the king, or a prince, but to him." She took another bite of her hamburger.

"You can be sure more than a few of them felt it when he died. Then to see him just being torn up and eaten? Yeah, they're scared now. They know if it can happen to their lord, it can happen to them."

What she said made Sean pause a moment.

"Do you think King Sladd felt it?" he asked her.

Estrella shrugged and swallowed what she'd been chewing on.

"Kind Sladd? I don't know, the lords aren't sworn directly to him. But Prince Talt?" Estrella nodded slowly. "Oh, I'm sure *he* felt it all right. When I killed that lord centuries ago, his prince knew about it almost instantly."

"Who is this Prince Talt?" Chad asked.

Sean grabbed another burger before answering.

"King Sladd has six princes. Each prince has a number of lords. The king gets power, magical power and I guess other things, from his princes.

His princes get it from their lords. Prince Talt owned the lord I killed today."

"And Prince Talt is?"

"King Sladd's A-Team," Sean said between bites.

Chad nodded. "Got it. Right, continuing on. With a six-mile front, it's going to be a lot harder now to stop them when the next push comes. But at least we know where they're all headed."

"We do?" Gloria asked.

"Reno, Mom," Roxy said.

"Ah!"

"Know this," Chad continued, "I'm moving all our troops into these staging zones." Chad pulled out a laser pointer and highlighted the drawn formations on the big map against the wall. Sean could see he'd obviously been hard at work.

"I've also notified Roloff to get the dwarves mobilized and to watch for small groups trying to sneak past the city's defenses."

Roloff nodded as Chad mentioned his name.

"How long do you think we have?" Sean asked.

"I think we'll start seeing small groups of stragglers in a few days. I don't think their army will be able to get past ours for at least a week."

"The best Chad and I can project," Maitland said, speaking up, "is if they continue to reinforce at their current rate, we'll see a number of skirmishes over the next three days as they try to push further away from the gateway.

"We both agree we won't really be able to do much more than slow them down; the geometry of the situation allows them to attack any one spot with more force than we can defend. So we'll just slowly pull back and let them expand their holdings."

"However," Chad said, taking back over, "eventually they'll have enough of a force here that they're going to stop being happy with what we're letting them take, and they're going to form up for a full attack and advance on Reno."

Sean looked thoughtful for a moment. "How long before they overrun the ranch?"

"Three, maybe four days."

Sean noticed there were a lot of shocked expressions around the table.

"And this is why I got us an airfield to the south," Sean said, tapping on the table. "Evacuation starts *now*. Understand? That's an order. Move out all the supporting staff like we planned it. We'll leave a fuel depot and some mechanics here, as well as a small holding force. We can keep staging out of here for now, but in two days, I want all our logistics forces at Mindren-Tahoe Airport. We'll stage the troops out of the Guard base at Reno international for now, but *our* base is going to be at Mindren."

"Won't the mayor and the rest of the city council panic at that?" Peg asked.

"Don't care," Sean said with a shake of his head. "We'll defend Reno as long as we can, but let's be realistic here; you have a starving army looking at more food than they've ever dreamed of. The closer they get, the harder they're going to fight."

"Yeah," Chad said with a heavy sigh. "Sooner or later, Reno is going to fall. It's just not very defensible."

Vincent Powers, the liaison with the magic user councils, spoke up next.

"What should I tell the councils?"

"Anybody north of the city needs to move, and they need to move *now*," Chad replied.

"I've already told them they need to evacuate anybody who isn't part of the fight," Sean added. "Make sure they understand that unless they're bunking with the troops, where it's safe, they need to head south to Vegas, and they need to do it *tonight*."

Vincent nodded. "I'll make sure they get the message.

"What about Carson City?" Oak asked. "How long until they get that?"

"Fortunately there are several passes between here and Carson City they'll have to use if they want to bring any force to bear. We've only got one to the north of Lake Washoe, and an even more defensible one just north of Carson. Maitland and I are pretty confident we can hold Carson against the djevels."

"Carson City isn't the problem, however," Maitland said, looking around the table. "Once we lose our ability to contain the djevels, they can head in *any* direction. Salt Lake is to the east, and Sacramento is to the west, with innumerable towns between here and there, as well as to the north of us. While most of the djevels will probably want to concentrate on Reno because it's close, we're going to be fighting them all over."

"Which comes back to why we're moving to Mindren and not Reno for the long term," Sean said. "We're going to have a lot of our army in the field. They're going to need resupply daily. If we set up to do that out of Reno, when Reno falls, they're *all* screwed."

"What about flights out of other cities? Surely we're not the only ones fighting this war, are we?" Gloria asked.

"We're working on it," Chad said. "But right now, we *are* the only ones fighting this war. Everything is concentrated here, and focused here. It's changing, and will continue to change, but going to war isn't like flipping a switch. There's a lot to be done to ramp things up. We've got several million troops here now, but if Estrella's estimates are correct, we're going to need millions more."

Sean raised his hand, stopping all conversation.

"Okay, I think we've heard enough about that. We need to get back to what's important, the evacuation. Now, Oak, Roxy, I know you've started on this already with the gear that was sent south. Let's get a priority list together and get cracking!"

Sean watched as everyone nodded, and he let Roxy take over. He knew Roxy and Oak had worked out a pretty detailed plan; they'd all just thought they had a few more weeks before they'd have to implement it.

But such were the fortunes of war.

§

"So my daughter tells me you killed a demon lord today?" Keairra asked, walking over to Sean as he woke up in the lion dreamland.

"Yes, and please don't hit me," Sean grumbled.

Keairra laughed. "What makes you think I was going to hit you?"

"Because your daughter almost did? Seriously, doesn't anybody trust me?"

"Not really," the First said, padding over to them. "You're still young yet, and you have to admit, you do have a tendency to go off half-cocked at times."

"Well, Stell beat one once, and I've beaten her, so I figured I had a good chance."

"You only beat her because you cheated," Keairra pointed out.

"Like I wasn't going to cheat against him?" Sean blew a raspberry. "Please! I'll cheat outrageously every time I'm presented the chance and my life is on the line."

"So what brings you here tonight?" the First asked.

Sean rolled his eyes and sighed. "You know, I do come here just to visit most of the time, even if this isn't one of them."

"Oh, don't feel bad," Keairra said with a laugh. "Estrella ratted you out."

Sean nodded. "When the lord died, I absorbed his power; I even absorbed him. Just like when I was in the Onderwereld."

"So?" the First asked. "That's why when one of us kills a demon, they don't reincarnate."

"The thing is, I felt it! I *learned* things from him!" Sean said, looking back and forth between them. "I'm not a demon, and I'm not on their plane. I know when we kill them we stop them from coming back, but I never actually *felt* it before."

The First shrugged. "The lords have a lot of power tied up in them; I'm not surprised you felt it."

"But, why?" Sean asked, looking confused.

"Why did you feel it? Or why do we absorb their power?"

"Why do we absorb their power? How does that happen? We're not demons!"

"Why can we do any of the things we can do?"

"Because you and Mom over there ate what's-his-name, Mahkiyoc's friend."

The First nodded. "Exactly. Why that is, I can't tell you. Somehow when we digested him, we got his abilities, and I guess his powers, as well."

Sean nodded slowly and sighed. "And that brings me to the next point; we need to go back to where that alien was and see if he managed to find anything on those weapons they used."

"Yes, we've gathered you're rather strong on that idea," Keairra said.

"I want to take as many of the other lions with me as possible."

"That's going to be a problem," the First said.

"We need those weapons, Dad! Also, if we're running around back there, we can do all sorts of things to mess them up. Kill their leaders, threaten them on their own ground. Disrupt them."

"Back before we knew how any of this worked, I thought that was a good idea," the First said. "But you found out for yourself how hard a lord is to kill. Can you imagine trying to kill a prince? Or worse yet, a king?"

"Could you kill a prince?" Sean asked the First.

"Yes, I believe I killed one once before. Those of us in my original pride, the First Pride, all of us know about the lords; we killed a lot of them the last time they tried to invade us. Back when we decided not to let them do it anymore.

"Well, back then, we came across one of their leaders who looked different from the other lords, and he was a lot tougher. We fought the entire night, then the day, and into the next night before I won. We had no idea then what he was. But now that I know…" the First shrugged. "I think I could do it again, but the problem is, I'm not alive down on Earth. Only a few of the First Pride are.

"Which brings me back to your request, Son. We have less than ten thousand lions living on the Earth now. Most all of them are engaged with important tasks. I can't just pull them from their current fights and send them to aid you in yours."

"But this is important, Dad! Weapons that kill djevels. If we can mass produce it, or even just copy it in limited numbers, we could quickly cut their numbers down to size."

The First pondered that a moment, nodding his head slightly. "Maybe after we've closed the permanent gate, we could do it. Then at least we wouldn't be risking as much."

"I can't wait that long." Sean sighed.

"Why not?"

"Because lately, I'm starting to realize, win or lose, if we do this the way we've planned, we're not going to have much of a world left when the smoke finally clears."

"It's better to have something left in the end than nothing left at all," the First pointed out.

"I'd rather have everything left at the end." Sean sighed. "Just accepting fate isn't something I'm very good at, Father."

"Well, the war is just starting. Let's see how it goes over the next month, as the gateways stabilize. We can talk about it again then."

Sean grumbled a little, but there wasn't much else he could say right then. He didn't have the equipment or the supplies for a trip yet, anyway. He'd hoped the First would be a lot more interested in the idea than he apparently was. So for now, he'd just have to wait and do a little lobbying while he got things together. He did still have one ace up his sleeve that he hadn't played yet.

Maybe when the opportunity came to use it, he could change the First's mind.

Wherever You Are

Sean woke up early for a change, someone having shifted in bed. That was when he noticed that Peg was getting up. He didn't say anything, just watched as she went over to one of the cribs, where their daughter Sharon was fussing.

Picking her up, Peg held Sharon to her breast, and the baby started nursing as she softly hummed a little tune. There were six cribs in the room, one for each of the children he'd had with his wives—well except for Jolene's twins Nguvu and Mtawala, they shared a slightly larger crib for now.

He just laid there quietly and watched Peg, without moving, enjoying the moment. He was a father now, and he'd come to appreciate these rare moments of calm and quiet. Between these seven, plus Deidre and Sheila's children, it was often noisy and chaotic when all his kids were around.

There were occasions when he wished he could spend more time with them, but he had a job to do if they were going to have any kind of a world to grow up in.

As he watched, each of his wives got up in turn as their babies woke. Roberta was next with their daughter Roseanne, then Roxy and Sean Junior, Daelyn and Bernard, Jolene and their two sons, and Cali last of all for Alska, their daughter.

"When's my turn?" Estrella whispered huskily in Sean's ear as her hand slowly slid down his chest towards his groin.

"After we get back from visiting Mahkiyoc," Sean said with a slight growl, "and trust me when I tell you, I hate waiting."

"I really don't want to go back there, but you're right, I'm the one who knows it. Just don't get me stuck there again."

Rolling over on top of her, Sean took her head between his hands and kissed her. "Don't worry. I know how to get us out of there, even if we can't get to a gate."

"Oh? And how is that?" Estrella asked, reaching around to grab those nice, muscular buns of his. She really did have a thing for his butt. Of course, she liked the other parts of him quite a bit as well, especially that one part she was urging him to slide up inside her.

"Promise not to tell your mom? Or your dad?" Sean asked.

"Why?"

"Because I know your dad, he lived in my head long enough, and I'm sure he'll find some reason to tell me why it can't be done."

"Then maybe you should listen to him?"

Sean snorted and ran his hands slowly down her body. "I only listen to him when he's right, and even then, I make him prove it. He's a tyrant, and while I love him like my very own father —" Sean paused a moment as he moved to kiss his way down her neck towards her chest, "hell, he *is* my father now—But he's still a tyrant, and there are times when…" Sean stopped as he reached a nipple and then gave it a slight nip, making Estrella gasp. "When he has to have the facts rubbed in his face before he'll have an *honest* discussion."

Estrella shivered and slid one hand up his back to run her fingers through his hair as he went back to teasing her nipple with his teeth. "Oh, don't stop! And you're right, he is. I won't tell."

"Promise?" Sean mumbled and gave her another nip, which made her shiver again.

"I prom...promise!" she groaned as his left hand discovered her damp sex and tickled things down there ever so slightly.

"I'm going to open a gate to la-la land."

Estrella blinked, but before she could formulate a response, he slid further down and stuck his tongue in her belly button, something that never failed to get a rise out of her.

"What?" she gasped after she stopped bucking against him. Sean was back to moving down her body.

"It's on the list of powers," Sean told her as he stopped at his destination and eyed the nice prize awaiting him.

"List of powers?"

"Yes. But it's expensive. Once there are enough lycans, I'll open one from here to prove it works."

"Prove wha..." Estrella's voice cut off as Sean dove into her sex, putting his tongue, teeth, and fingers to very good use. She grabbed his hair with both hands and wrapped her legs around him as she held on. Apparently the other wives had trained him well, because damn if breathing and holding on were the only things she could think about!

Sean snickered as Estrella wrapped herself around him and went to town on her. All of his women were very responsive to oral sex, and he enjoyed giving it as much as they enjoyed receiving. He spent a good long while licking, nipping, and pinching her through a couple of well-deserved orgasms before her grip loosened enough that he was able to lick his chops and kiss his way back up her body.

Rubbing his erect shaft over her now soaked lower lips, he settled in between her legs.

"You...you said a, a gate?" Estrella asked as her eyes slowly focused. Reaching down, she took Sean's manhood into her hand and led him to her entrance. She was definitely ready to take her mate inside her body once more.

Sean grunted as he slid deep into familiar depths once more. "Yes," he whispered as he kissed her again and slowly licked his way up to her left ear.

"How?" Estrella said and tried to evade his approaching lips. Tickling her ear always drove her crazy, and while she might secretly enjoy it, she'd never tell *him* that.

"It's on the list."

"What..." Estrella shivered as his tongue started in on her ear.

Sean snickered as Estrella wrapped her legs around him as his hips began to move his shaft in and out of her tight heat, while her hands vainly tried to pull his head away from the teasing his tongue was now doing.

"...list?" Estrella growled, and tried to focus on the conversation instead of the wonderful feelings going through her body.

Relenting a moment, Sean's raised his head. "The list of our powers."

"I...where is this list?"

"In our heads," Sean said and, looking up, he noticed the others were giving him the eye.

"I don't have a list in my head!" Estrella panted.

"Jo, could you join us?" Sean said, and then smiling down at Estrella, he added, "Why don't we fix that?"

"Huh?"

Sean rolled over onto his back, pulling Estrella along with him.

"What's up, Sean?" Jolene asked as she climbed up onto the bed with them.

"I want to teach Estrella some spells," Sean told her, grabbing Estrella's hips as she sat up to straddle him. Estrella reached around to tickle his balls as she started to shimmy and grind down against him. She didn't mind sharing—she was a lioness after all—and Jolene really was a doll.

"She's not a magic user," Jolene said as she leaned over and kissed Sean, putting a hand on each of them.

"This is *lion* magic," Sean told her as she broke the kiss.

Jolene smiled and gave a small shrug, then turning her attention to Estrella, she gave her a warm kiss as she moved to straddle Sean's body.

Sean didn't hesitate. Moving his hands to cup Jolene's generous chest, he urged her backwards until he could put his tongue to good use on her as Estrella rode his body, making her own needs quite clear.

Jolene sighed as Sean went to work, pulling Estrella closer into her embrace, letting her hands explore Estrella's body as Estrella did the same to her. Closing her eyes, she kissed Estrella and opened up her magic. She'd been in both of their heads often enough at this point that it wasn't difficult; she did 'feed' her magic off of all of them, after all.

'*This way,*' Sean's thoughts sent to her, and as she got comfortable in his head, he pulled her down towards the old learning aid spell he'd gotten from his father's books.

'*I still don't see how she can use this,*' Jolene said.

'*I'll show you were to put it.*'

'*I'm sure you will!*' Jolene teased. Looking it over, she copied it and then flowed into Estrella's mind, with Sean watching where she was going.

Estrella continued to drive Sean's shaft in and out of her body as she watched inside her head as Jolene *explored* her. It was quite stimulating; apparently mind magic always was, which was why tantric witches were so good at it.

When Jolene finally stopped at a place inside her, she shivered as she heard Sean's voice inside her head.

'*Put it there.*'

Jolene looked around, surprised. There was power here, alright, but a kind of power she'd never seen before, and one she wasn't willing to experiment with touching. How she'd never noticed it before was beyond her; maybe because Sean was now working with her?

In either case, she carefully copied the spell into Estrella's mind, then checking her work over quickly, she pulled back out until she was only in deep enough to feed.

Between Estrella's fingers—which had moved back to teasing him—the way she was grabbing at him with her insides while she rode him like a bucking bronc, and of course Jolene's mind magic, Sean didn't last much longer at that point.

Neither did Estrella, and even Jolene joined them as they all climaxed together, a heaving, sweaty, panting, and quite satisfied tangle of three bodies.

"Gee, that looks like fun, Lion-boy!" Daelyn laughed. "My turn!"

"Don't forget me this time, either!" Roberta snickered.

"I live to please," Sean said with a happy smile. Sometimes getting up early was worth it.

It was much later in the day when Estrella caught up with Sean, who was helping Roxy, Daelyn, and Oak go over the last of the evacuation plans. She'd been busy herself helping get the children ready to go. Most of the non-essential personal had started moving out a couple of days ago, but Sean had decreed last night that they would all be moved out by sunset today.

So things around the ranch were fairly busy.

"Sean, do you have a minute?" she asked, coming into the room.

Sean looked up from the diagram he was studying. "Sure, Stell, what's up?"

"That 'thing' you put in me this morning..."

"Is that anyway to talk about a man's dick?" Daelyn asked with a smirk, causing Roxy and Sean both to start laughing.

Blushing, Estrella growled at Daelyn, "That's not what I'm talking about, and you should know it! Sean had Jo copy some sort of spell into my head!"

Daelyn laughed. "It was still worth it to see you blush! Damn, you're a hard one to get, Stell! Now I get to see how much I won!"

"Won? What are you talking about?"

"They have a pot going on who can make you blush first," Sean said. "Though for some reason, I'm excluded from the betting."

Estrella blushed again. "You're kidding me?" she said in a much lower voice.

"Course not," Roxy said, smiling. "Sean makes you blush all the time! That's why he's not allowed in it. I mean he just made you blush again, am I right?"

Estrella tried to scowl at Roxy as she continued blushing. "Is there an award for second place, too?"

"Nah, that one was just because I could!" Roxy laughed.

Smiling, Sean came around the table, took Estrella by the elbow, and steered her towards the door. "Let's find someplace a little less distracting, and I'll show you how to use it."

"Don't be gone too long!" Roxy called out. "We still have to get this finished!"

Sean nodded and lead Estrella out of Roxy's office, closing the door behind them.

"Sorry about that," Sean said with a smile, "but it *was* funny."

"It's okay. It's nice that they're finally starting to treat me the same way they treat each other. I know it's taken me a while to get used to all the changes. Though," she looked at Sean, "a wager on who could get me to blush?"

"You should see the side pot on who would win it!" Sean said with a chuckle. "I had a hundred on Dae, so I think it's safe to say I just doubled my money, at least."

"Why Dae?"

"Because she's rude, crude, and not afraid of you in a fight. She may be small, but she's deadly!"

Estrella sighed, but had to smile. "Yeah, dwarves are like that. So, how do I use this thing you put in my head?"

Sean steered her into his office, which was a lot smaller than Roxy's. Peg wasn't there currently; she was busy helping get the kids moved.

"Okay, how do you currently use your lion powers?"

Estrella shrugged. "Mostly I just think about them. Mom trained me. She told me what they are, how they 'feel', and what to expect from them. It took me a while to get the hang of it, but over time, I got each of them down."

Sean nodded. "Okay, try doing the same thing, only this time, think about opening up your 'stats' menu."

"Stats menu?" she asked, looking at him.

"This spell is about looking at your statistics." Sean walked over to the whiteboard and picked up a marker. "Magic users use it to find out what their physical stats are, their mental ones, and then they go down to the list of spells. It looks like this."

Sean made a list on the white board; under the heading of 'Physical', he listed: Constitution, Agility, Strength, and Regeneration. Then he put the heading 'Mental' up and listed: Intelligence, Wisdom, Reasoning, Memory, and Integration. Last he put up 'Magical', and under that: Ability, Mana, and Will.

"Now, this first group," he said pointing to physical, "deals with your body, obviously. Some of these you can change, some you can't. The first three all magic users get; the forth one is only for us lycans. Magic users don't even see that one," Sean said taping the tip of the marker by 'Regeneration'.

"The second group is your mental abilities; again, some you can affect, some you can't."

"What's 'integration'? I think the others are obvious."

"That's another lycan skill magic users don't get to see. It's how well your two halves are integrated with each other.

"The last three on the third heading are all about magical abilities; I don't know if you'll see any of those. Heck, I don't know if you'll see *any* of this, because this is all magic user stuff, and we can use our experiences to make changes in most of these numbers."

"Then why did you give it to me?" Estrella asked.

Sean smiled. "Because for me, the memory stat," Sean circled it on the whiteboard, "has a tab under it that I can open up and see *all* the lion powers."

"So that's this 'list' you keep talking about?"

Sean nodded. "I don't know if I was missing it when dad was in my head, or if he was hiding it from me. But after he was kicked out, I saw a little drop-down marker, and I opened it up, and there it all was in a great big list."

"How big?"

"Well, it was broken up into three headings. One had to do with languages, one had to do with the mystical shit we get to do..."

"You mean leonine powers," Estrella interrupted, rolling her eyes.

Sean grinned. "Yeah, mystical shit. The third was our Status. It told how much power there was, how much I had saved up, the number of lycans currently alive, and the number of lions currently alive."

"So that's how Dad always knows how many lycans are alive!" she said, surprised.

"From talking with Dad, I'm not sure he experiences this the way I do. He told me he had to learn it all by pretty much just guessing and messing around with it. Magic users created a spell for their abilities, and I guess the spell just latched onto it, because it's a similar kind of thing."

Estrella nodded. "Okay, that makes sense. Well, let me give it a try."

Leaning back in the seat and closing her eyes, she concentrated on the idea of a list of abilities like Sean had put on the board.

Almost immediately, three words appeared to her: Statistics, Abilities, and Languages.

"I can see them!" she said, surprised.

"What does it say?"

"Well, the order is different, and so are the words. It says Statistics, Abilities, and Languages."

Sean 'hmmmed' at that. "Well, that's interesting. Then again, I've never done this with anyone else before, so it may be sorted by some unconscious preference of your own. Try selecting Statistics and see what happens."

Estrella did so, and immediately the same three items Sean had mentioned before dropped down.

"There're over five *million* lycans now! Oh, wow...."

"Five million, two hundred and ninety-six thousand, four hundred and twenty-three."

"Now twenty-seven," Estrella said and watched as the number continued to climb. "Someone's busy!"

"Yeah, we are, everywhere," Sean agreed. "Now, go to 'Abilities'."

Estrella looked at the very long list of things that quickly dropped down. "Wow, I know most of these! And you're saying I can improve them?"

"You can put power into them, so yes, you can improve them, but it's not as simple as that. For some things, you have to work at them and practice them while putting the power in."

Estrella scrolled down, looking for the word 'gateway'.

"I can't find the gateway thing you're talking about, Sean."

"Try looking under 'visit'."

It only took her a moment. There it was, 'Visit Leonine World'. The incorporeal skill had two numbers after it. It appeared to have a lot more power in it than it needed, and she said so.

"That's because you opened it when we were in the djevel's world," Sean told her.

"Oh, that makes sense." She looked at the corporeal skill then.

"It's almost four million points!" she blurted out.

"Yup, and look at the point pool in your statistics tab."

Estrella did, and she noticed it was over three million now, though it didn't stay very steady, constantly moving up and down.

"It's close," she told him, opening her eyes and looking at him, the numbers and abilities still floating before her eyes. With a thought, she canceled the spell.

"If no one was using their power, we'd have more than enough, but I don't want to burn the whole pool, so I'm waiting until we've got more power."

"And then what? You'll open a gate?"

Sean nodded. "Of course I will! And then I'm going to drag Dad's ass through it so he's here with the rest of us. We have more than enough lycans now, as I understand it, for all those on the other plane to come here and help us! Think about it, twenty thousand more lions!"

"I'm sure he has a good reason," Estrella said.

"And if he doesn't?"

Estrella growled, "Then I'll help you drag his ass through myself!"

"Just remember, don't bring this up to him yet."

"Why?"

"Better to plead ignorance than to beg forgiveness after being told 'no'."

Estrella opened her mouth to make a comment about that, then suddenly blushed as she recalled doing the exact same thing when she'd gone through that gate so many centuries ago.

"I knew you'd see it my way!" Sean said with a smile, and getting up, he leaned over and kissed her. "I need to get back to work."

"Will you be traveling with us tonight?"

Sean nodded. "There's no way I'm going to let my wives and children make that trip without me there guarding all of you."

Estrella smiled. "See you later, Love."

Escalation

"Turn left here and cut across yon field," Bilkie said.

Karl nodded, turned the wheel on the Fennek, and adjusted the tire pressure with his left hand. He then engaged the four-wheel drive system as they plowed through the closed gate and continued forward on their course.

"Anybody see anything?" Karl called over the intercom to the back, were Otto was sitting up in the open gunner's position, and two others, another werewolf and a mage they'd borrowed, were sitting in the passenger's compartment below.

"I'm impressed by your memory," Karl said as they bounced over the field. They were retracing the path Bilkie and the other Kitesh Korps had taken during their flight from Berlin. It was probably safer than going through any of the towns, a fair deal of which were now almost completely abandoned.

The Fennek was a fairly quiet vehicle made for exactly this kind of job. It was fast, and actually fairly comfortable on the paved roads, and the ride off-road wasn't as bad as it could have been. Still, it had been over a decade since he'd driven one. But because he *had* driven one, when the time came to send someone out to do reconnaissance, Raban had been quick to 'volunteer' Karl for the job.

Karl had thought long and hard about telling Raban off, but Otto had told him that arguing with lions was often messy business.

'What do you mean by *messy*?' Karl had asked.

'Well, when they bite your head off, the blood does seem to go everywhere!'

Karl shook his head and sighed. He didn't think Raban would go that far, but whether he liked it or not, Raban trusted him, and he knew the territory. He also got on quite well with the Kitesh Korps people. So well that he was now living with them. Sure, they were all crooks, and he was a cop, but that just meant that they had a lot more in common with each other than the average citizen.

"Nothing from up here!" Otto called down, breaking Karl out of his revery.

"Truth be told," Bilkie said with a chuckle. "If what Raban thinks is true and there really are just a few small bands running around to scare everyone off, we won't be findin' anything until we get to Berlin."

"Good thing we're not going to Berlin then, isn't it?" Karl replied.

"Still," Otto said, "he does want an idea of how far out they're ranging."

"Yes, well, if he's lucky and we're lucky, we might be able to tell him that, but I'm not getting within sixty kilometers of the outskirts."

"There's a hill to the north of us," Otto said. "Maybe we should head up there and get a good look ahead of us before we make our way down to the road to cross the Elbe?"

"Sure, why not? If it looks safe, maybe we can get out for a few minutes and stretch our legs."

"Oh, that would be a blessin'!" Bilkie said with a sigh. "We've been in this metal beast for way too many hours!"

Karl turned the Fennek and headed up the hill. He parked just a few yards shy of the top. No reason to make it obvious to everyone he was there. It'd be just his luck if there was still a higher-ranking member of the police around who might try to commandeer him or his vehicle.

After he'd parked, Otto and Jegel, the other wolf, went out and did a search of the area around them first, to make sure it was safe. Once the 'all clear' was called, they got out and stretched for a bit, Jurgen, their magic user, relieving himself on a nearby bush.

Karl found his own bush, then walked up to the top of the rise, where Otto and Bilkie were looking off in the distance with binoculars.

"See anything?"

"Not really, the town down by the river looks deserted. I guess people either fled or died," Otto said.

"What's that?" Jurgen asked, pointing up into the sky.

"What's what?" Karl asked, and everyone looked up. Off in the distance, way off in the distance, there were a bunch of contrails quickly streaking towards the ground. Karl suddenly got a very bad feeling.

"Everyone back in the truck! NOW!"

"I wonder where they're..." Karl grabbed Jurgen by the arm and hauled him off to the Fennek.

"Look away! Don't look at it!"

They'd just reached the vehicle when a bright flash appeared behind them. Fortunately they were behind the hill already. He didn't think they'd be in direct line of sight—Berlin was still almost a hundred kilometers away—but he still remembered all the drills they'd had to do back when he'd done his tour of duty in the military.

"What was that?"

"Someone just dropped several nuclear bombs on Berlin!" Karl said and, getting inside, he fired up the engine as the others followed.

"Close the door! Close the hatch! Seal up everything!"

"Won't we suffocate?" Bilkie asked.

"This thing has filters, we'll be fine."

"From what?" Jurgen asked.

"Fallout."

Karl spun the vehicle around and floored it. If someone was dropping warheads from orbit, the last place he wanted to be was near anything that could be a target.

"Otto! Get on the radio, call Raban, tell him what we just saw."

"Immediately," Otto agreed.

As they came down the hill, Karl glanced out the window in the direction of Berlin. There were multiple fireballs rising up over the city as the mushroom clouds formed. Too many to count at this distance.

"Do you think it was the Americans, or the Russians?" Jegel asked.

"Neither, I'd guess," Otto said with a shake of his head as he tried to raise someone back in Munich on the radio. "I don't think they'd have used more than one; I'm fairly certain their missiles have much larger warheads on them."

"How many do ya' think there were?" Bilkie asked.

"More than six," Karl said as he continued to drive.

"Do you think it killed the demons?" Jurgen asked.

"I think someone other than us can answer that question. I'm not immune to radiation, and neither are you. Otto? Bilk?"

"I'm not," Bilkie said.

"I think werewolves are," Otto said a little uncomfortably, "but I'd rather not put it to the test."

"Me neither," Jegel agreed.

Karl raised the tire pressure as they hit the road, shifted back to two-wheel drive, and floored it. Most of the roads coming here had been clear, and the Fennek could do a hundred kph easily. He wanted to get as far from here as he could, in case whoever was doing the shooting decided on another round. With sunset only a few hours away, he wanted to make as much use of the daylight as he could.

#

"The French just nuked Berlin!"

"What?" Sean said, looking up from his breakfast. It was just after eight, and he hadn't gotten to sleep until almost four. Moving everyone and getting their new living quarters set up in one of the newly constructed buildings last night had taken a lot more time than he'd expected.

Right now he was eating breakfast in the new 'mess', along with pretty much everyone else.

Oak said again, "The French nuked Berlin! It's on the news! They used one of their subs to do it. Dropped like ten warheads on the city; there's nothing left, it's like a big hole in the ground! One of the independent satellite mapping companies just put up a picture!"

"Why the hell would the *French* of all people nuke Berlin?" Sean asked, looking around the room.

Roxy's father Bill answered him, "After being invaded and conquered in two World Wars, the French developed a very progressive belief on self defense when they became worried about the Russians doing it a third time. So they made a rule that if anything made it to the Fulda Gap, they'd launch all their nukes. I guess this qualified."

"Well, if the French are doing it, I don't think we have to worry about the president giving us the weapons so we can do it here, too," Daelyn said as she fed Bernard.

"But the French?" Sean said, looking surprised.

"Don't sell the French short," Bill said. "They're a lot tougher than most folks realize. At least their military is."

"I wonder if the djevels will be coming back from that one or not?" Roxy mused.

"Depends on if there were any lions around to suck up their souls when they died, if I understand it right," Sean said.

"I don't think a lion can withstand a nuclear blast anymore than the rest of us, Sean!"

Sean shook his head slowly. "I dunno. If they were in something that could protect them from the fireball, they just might. But I don't think they'd be in any kind of shape to do anything for a while."

"Is this the voice of personal experience?" Roxy asked with a growl and looked at Estrella, who just shrugged.

"It's not anything I'd want to repeat, like ever," Sean said with a shudder. "It hurt. And when I came to, it continued to hurt. But the rules are different there, so I don't know if that would work here or not."

"Hopefully this means Raban and the others in Munich have a chance now," Estrella said. "Most of the djevels were in Berlin, after all. If this killed them, it gives the people fighting in Europe much better odds for survival."

"I just wonder if the demons know what happened, and what they'll do to stop it from happening again?"

Bill shrugged. "No use borrowing trouble, we got enough of our own already."

Sean stood up. "Well, I need to meet with Samis about a few things, but right now I think I need to call Steve and get an idea of what's going on in DC."

Sean gave each of his wives a kiss, and his kids a pat on the head, and found a quiet spot to call Steve.

"Wow, you're up early," Steve said, answering the phone.

"We moved last night, and the kids are taking their sweet time with settling into the new surroundings. Sleep isn't something I got a lot of last night," Sean explained with a sigh. "Now, obviously you know why I'm calling?"

"Yeah, I would have called you earlier if I knew you were awake. But right now it's not like we can do anything."

"So why the hell did France nuke Berlin?"

"Because they weren't going to wait for a consensus or ask for anyone's opinion."

"What?"

Steve laughed. "That's what they said. They said 'Berlin was a problem, everyone knew it, and rather than sit around with panicked expressions and laments of fear, they dealt with the problem decisively, and once everyone has calmed down, the French government is sure cooler heads will not only agree it was the right thing to do, but will thank the French government for this bold and necessary action.'"

"They said *that*?" Sean asked, surprised.

"Almost word for word."

"And how are people reacting to it?"

"Well, after Tisha, the president, and I had a *very* unexpected meeting an hour ago, where Tisha went into some detail about what was going on in Berlin, the United States officially sided with France. Interestingly enough, Britain, Austria, and Belgium sided with them before that, and everyone else in the area added their support within the hour. Even the Russians are now praising France for its decisiveness."

"So just how many did they drop?"

"Ten three hundred kiloton warheads."

"Ten?"

"Their submarine-launched missiles are apparently the shit. The Pentagon folks were raving over their accuracy. They laid down a five-pointed star pattern, with five on the star points, and another five on the points where the lines cross, basically a pentagon within a pentacle, and they all went off at the exact same time. I tell ya', if the Russians were ever thinking of invading France, they just got one hell of a wake-up call!" Steve said and laughed again.

"I guess I'm going to have to talk to my people to see how all the non-humans we've got heading over there to join the fight feel about this new development." Sean sighed and shook his head. "Glad it's not *my* headache!"

"Terri's parents called last night and said you evacuated the Reno Stead airport?"

"Yup. The commercial folks were given twenty-four hours to get out. The Air Guard base should be gone already."

"So you're out of the Ranch now too?"

"Almost. We're still going to stage some of our forces out of it for now. But we're not going to waste anyone's life trying to hold it. You know, I haven't had the time to check, have your parents left Reno yet?"

"Yeah, Mom and Dad are in Vegas setting up a new shop. Dad dragged half the crew and all the older staff down there with him. Said the business in Reno was already dropping off. Once he gets that done, he's gonna come here and see about helping me open up a place in DC."

"That's not why I sent you out there, you know."

"Sure it was! You want to see my family empire increase! This whole 'deal with the president' thing was just a clever disguise! I can see that now!" Steve said, chuckling. "Besides, I now have a bunch of people who are just sitting on their butts all day. Time to give them something useful to do."

"Does that mean the ALS has been dealt with?"

"Oh, we're still dealing with them, but they've been cut back a lot. That guy who got arrested is coming up for trial soon, and he's been singing like a bird, to use an old phrase. Apparently he hasn't been doing well in the general population and had to be put into some sort of 'protective' holding."

"Your doing?" Sean asked, genuinely curious.

"Hell, no. I need that guy to be prosecuted for the PR value. But at least he's fingered several high-value targets, and the FBI's been taking them down, one by one. We're getting a lot of news value out of it here on the east coast."

"Well, if you can get a lead on their west coast leaders, let me know."

"What for?"

"They tried to bomb us, and I don't have time to deal with that kind of shit anymore. Tell me where they are, and *I'll* task somebody to go deal with them."

"That might cause some problems for us, Sean."

"Right now I'm more worried about someone blindsiding us while we're dealing with the djevels that will probably be attacking Reno a week or two from now."

Steve thought about that a moment. "You know what? I'll drop a few hints with the SS folks that they need to lean on the FBI to clean up the western operations of those jokers before they end up demon food."

"You might also tell them they need to start pulling their own people out of the high-risk areas. That, or assign them to me."

"I'll be sure to pass that on."

"Well, I got things to do, and I'm sure you do too. Give my love to Terri and Tisha."

"Right-o. Give my regards to Roxy and the rest."

"Bye."

Sean hung up and went back to the mess, where Daelyn was just finishing up.

"I need to go see your uncle and your friend Geris about all those weapons we ordered."

Daelyn nodded. "Give me time to clean up and I'll meet you out by the car in twenty. Cali!" Daelyn called.

"What, Dae?"

"We're going to my folks! Twenty minutes!"

"Got it!"

"You sure it's safe to bring her?" Sean asked, a little worried.

Daelyn growled. "The Carson City halls are *my* hometown. I've made it clear to everyone there that, as Cali is one of *my* sister wives, she damn well better be welcome there, or I'll be putting Maxwell up their ass!"

Sean nodded. "Sounds good then. I'll help the others get the kids settled, and I'll see you at the car in twenty."

Sean followed Daelyn and Cali through Geris' factory and into the office, where Geris and Samis were waiting for them today. Roxy had decided at the last minute to come along as well.

"Great to see you, Uncle," Daelyn said, giving Samis a hug, then she gave Geris one. "You too, Geris."

Roxy then did the same with Samis, but only shook hands with Geris, followed by Cali.

Sean was surprised that Samis didn't hesitate to give Cali a hug, and Geris was more than happy to shake hands with her. Sean followed up, shaking hands with both of them. As he was in his hybrid form, Geris looked at him a little surprised, but Samis had seen him like this several times now and didn't comment.

"Nice to see all of you," Geris said with a smile. "Now, let me show you what I've got."

Walking over to a large table with several firearms on it, Geris waved them over.

"First off," he said, picking up the first one and handing it to Sean, "repeating rifles. We went out and bought a bunch of forty-five seventy's, and then took some time to work on the action so it wouldn't gum up easily from the black-powder residue."

Sean looked at it and worked the action.

"Feels a little loose."

Geris nodded. "That's intentional. Black powder is pretty dirty, and repeating rifles need a lot of lube to keep them running well. For cleaning, you can pretty much just dunk them in water and not worry about it. By the time these start to rust, I suspect you'll be long gone from your destination."

Sean nodded and passed it on to Roxy, who immediately started looking it over quite carefully.

"Is there water over there, Sean?" Roxy mumbled.

"Actually, I have no idea," Sean admitted.

"Then we're going to need some stiff brushes with each of the rifles to keep the gunk from caking up too thick," she said, looking up at Geris, who just nodded.

Roxy then passed it on to Cali, who also gave it a thorough inspection, but she didn't add any comments.

"How may of them do you have?" Sean asked.

"Fifty of them. I can get you more if you wait longer, but with the current priority being supplying the people fighting here, I only have two people I can assign to work on this."

"Okay, what else do you have?"

Geris picked up a double-barreled shotgun and handed it to Sean. Sean looked it over. It was a lot shorter than a normal one; obviously the barrel had been shortened a fair deal.

"We thought about pump actions, but with black powder, we got worried about jamming issues. Double-barreled shotguns are pretty simple, easy to shoot, easy to load, easy to clean. We shortened them a bit to give a better spread pattern, as well."

Sean nodded and handed it to Roxy.

"How many of those do you have?"

Geris laughed. "How many do you want? They're so cheap we bought a couple thousand, and we've been handing them out to anybody and everybody who wants one. With iron pellet buckshot, these are hell on the demons. The only difference between you and the others is you'll be shooting black powder. We didn't have to change a thing on the shotguns."

"Sounds good. Now, sidearms?"

"We got a bunch of forty-four special pistols. They're not all the same; we really just went around and found what we could."

"Why forty-four?"

"Because it works well with black powder, and we didn't want the ammo getting confused with the forty-fives we've been giving the troops here. Plus revolvers were made with black powder in mind, and the rimmed cartridges of the forty-four special are easier to load."

Sean nodded and took the two pistols Geris handed him. He passed one on to Roxy immediately, and looked the other over for a moment, before passing it on to her as well. They weren't matched; one had a three-inch barrel, the other a five.

"Mostly we've got Rugers and Smith and Wessons," Geris continued. "But there are some Charter Arms and Colts in there as well. I daresay we'll have more trouble making holsters for whatever you pick than we'll have with getting pistols."

"Cowboy holsters," Roxy spoke up. "The type with webbing for bullets so we can reload quickly. For the shotguns and the rifles, we'll be slinging them on our backs, so we'll want bandoliers on the straps, and then just extra bandoliers that we can sling with ammo as well."

Sean blinked and looked over at Roxy, but didn't say anything.

"We'll get right on it," Geris said with a nod. "Shouldn't take more than a few days."

"What about ammo?" Sean said, looking at Samis.

"Other than having to be extra careful with the black powder, ammo isn't a problem, Sean," Samis said, motioning towards several large crates stacked by the wall. "We just finished a run of forty-five seventy, twenty thousand rounds, and another ten thousand of shotgun shells. We're going to run out another twelve thousand of the shotgun shells, and we should have twenty thousand pistol rounds done within the next three days."

Samis looked back at Sean. "Which leads to the question: How many people are going?"

Sean took a deep breath and sighed. "I'm not quite sure yet. We're thinking three teams going in, but we're not sure how many people we want on the other two. It's going to be about twenty with me, I think."

"So we should figure thirty on each team, or ninety total?"

Sean looked at Roxy and Cali, who both gave small nods. He agreed and said so, "Yeah, I think that'll work."

"Okay, I'll see if we can get any more of the rifles. It's the only long-range weapon you're going to have."

Roxy spoke up again, "See if you can find some rolling block rifles, or some breechblock rifles. There were a lot made in forty-five seventy. Ruger still makes them in breechblock. They were made to deal with black powder."

"Aren't those single shot?"

"That won't be an issue," Roxy assured him.

"Okay, I'll see what we can gather up," Geris said. "If we don't have to modify them to work with black powder, we should be able to get them quickly."

"Sounds good. Deliver what you've got now out to the airport. That'll give people time to get used to the weapons."

"When are you planning on going?" Samis asked.

Sean shook his head. "No idea. There's just too many variables right now. But I'd like to be ready by Monday, the twelfth."

"That only gives us four days," Geris warned.

Sean nodded. "I know, I know. But I want to be ready by then in case the opportunity presents itself."

"Okay, I'll ship everything we've got over this afternoon."

"Great, thanks."

"I still think you're crazy for wanting to go back there, Sean," Samis said.

Sean shrugged. "They had weapons that could kill the djevels so they wouldn't come back. We need that. Besides, they don't think we can touch them. With the other two groups running around and attacking them, it'll definitely be a wake up and might just take the pressure off here for a while."

"Especially if we can kill some of their leaders," Roxy added.

"Well, good luck, and don't do anything stupid," Samis told Sean. "None of us want to lose you, Sean. You're family now."

Sean smiled. "Thanks, I appreciate it."

Shaking hands again, they left and headed back to the car. Once they were out of the factory, Sean stopped and turned to look at Roxy.

"We? What's this 'we' shit?" he said, almost growling.

Roxy smiled sweetly at him and then kicked him in the balls! Sean's eyes went wide and Roxy grabbed his mane and pulled his head down until it was level with hers.

"I'm going. Cali's going. Peg is going. Estrella's going. And you better get used to that idea, or you're most certainly *not* going."

Sean blinked as her words blindsided him. This wasn't anything he'd been expecting.

Daelyn spoke up, "We had this conversation yesterday while you were busy, Lion-boy. Who could go, and who couldn't. Roxy and Peg are lycans; we know they won't be affected. Cali's a dark elf; we know they're not affected either.

"I'm staying home to run things and keep whatever lion you leave behind on the straight and narrow, with Jolene and Roberta to help me keep an eye on our children."

"What if I say no?" Sean asked. He didn't growl it out, but he still wasn't sure he liked it.

Daelyn pulled out a pair of battery-powered shears. "Then we're going to shave you bald, kitty cat."

And damned if Cali and Roxy didn't each pull out a set as well.

Sighing and shaking his head, Sean gave Roxy a kiss. Then after she let go, Cali and Daelyn as well.

"I guess I'm outvoted."

"And still furry!" Cali teased. "Which pleases me greatly, I don't know if I'd like to see my husband bald."

"Yeah, sounds cold," Sean agreed as they got into the 'Cuda.

"And Peg was alright with this?" he asked after a minute's thought.

"At first she wasn't sure she wanted to go," Roxy told him, "but she changed her mind last night."

"Oh? Why?"

"Because she didn't think one magic user would be enough."

"What about Stewart?"

"We think he should go with one of the other groups, Husband," Cali said.

"It's too bad we don't have more magic users we could send," Roxy said with a sigh of her own. "But lycan magic users aren't very common, and no one's been willing to take Peg up on her offer to convert them."

"Well, it's only worked twice that we know of," Sean said.

"Actually, there's a third time, Husband," Cali said with a wink. "But we promised not to tell you about it."

Sean just shook his head and rolled his eyes. "I'm sure I really don't want to know."

Grand Designs

Steve walked into the small room and immediately collapsed back against the wall, panting.

"What's wrong?" Tisha asked, coming into the room next and going over to him.

"When I thought this would be a good idea, I had no idea just how *badly* some of these people were injured!" Steve took a moment to catch his breath. "And then there's what you and the others had to do to make them right, to heal them, when you were infecting them!

"All that blood! The limbs! It's worse than the shootout on the highway!"

Tisha gave him a hug. "I had no idea it was bothering you, Steve."

Steve sighed and hugged her back. "It wasn't. *At first*. But after the sixth one? How do you manage? Hell, how do Granite and the others manage?"

"Because we've seen it all before."

"You I can believe," Steve said. "You're a lioness, you've been around, you've seen and experienced more than I probably ever will. You've been to war and fought with swords, while I've grown up in a much safer world. But Granite, the other wolves, they grew up in the same world, but they don't even flinch."

"Now you know what Sean was saving us from," Granite said, having followed Tisha into the room. "Because the lives we lived before he came and saved us really were worse than this."

"How does Sean even manage?"

"Because he's a lion?" Granite said with a shrug. "Honestly, the fact that you held it together until we were done impressed everyone out there. They could tell you weren't comfortable; hell, we could smell it," Granite said with a disarming laugh. "But you still stuck it out with the rest of us."

"I'm your leader; I'm the guy in charge. I *owe* it to you," Steve said with a repressed shudder. "It wouldn't be right for me to dump all of that on you."

"Next time, you will," Tisha told him. "They're all impressed that you did your part, but there's no reason to be here for this anymore."

"It's not their opinion I'm worried about," Steve said with a sigh.

"Oh? Is it mine, then?"

Steve snorted and looked into Tisha's eyes with a grin. "No, it's mine. My opinion. I don't like asking people to do things and run off when they get nasty. You're my team, my people. If I don't weather the storms with you, how can I really say I know who you are? People are forged by a common experience, and you're *my* people. That makes you my responsibility; you're all my hopes, my dreams, my successes, and yes, even my failures. I have to own this, all of it."

Tisha smiled then and, leaning forward, she tilted her head up and kissed him.

"And my mother wonders why I turned down all those other males for you! You're more of a lion than my last ever was!"

"Please, don't tell me I now have to battle your six evil exes!" Steve joked.

"Nope. But if you did, I'm sure you'd win."

Steve turned and looked over at Granite. "Do we have enough space for all our new friends, or do I need to rent a hotel?"

"We're going to shuffle them between Card's group over at Sapientia and Race's people over at Eruditio. It's well away from any outside influences, and there's a lot of nice open space in the area for them to run while they learn about their new bodies."

Steve nodded. "I guess once they're over the shock, we can send them home or back to the military, or wherever it is they have to go. I'll talk to the doctors."

"I'll get them organized," Granite said with a nod and left.

"Come, let's get this over with," Steve said and led Tisha out of the room.

"Ah! Steven! I was just looking for you!" said Doctor Carella, the director of the hospital, coming up to them in the hallway.

"Well, it's a good thing you found me then," Steve said with an easy smile, putting the day's experiences behind him, for now. "I wanted to let you know we're going to be taking all those we infected today with us, so we can spend a few days teaching them about their new abilities before sending them back."

Doctor Carella nodded. "That does make sense. People often forget that physical therapy is important after you recover from a serious injury. But that's not the reason I was looking for you."

"Oh?" Steve asked, curious.

"Well, you see, we have a *lot* of outpatients in the DC area. And then of course, there are the other veteran's hospitals, and, well, a few of the generals from the Pentagon called after they heard about the successes you were having here, and we were all wondering..." the doctor asked, giving Steve a hopeful look.

"Of course we will!" Steve said with a cheerful smile that was only partially faked. "I'll even talk to my boss about setting up teams to go around to the different hospitals. Just make sure everyone understands that not everyone can be made whole again, for all that we'll do what we can."

Doctor Carella smiled broadly then and stuck out his hand, which Steve shook.

"Oh, trust me, I know there are no guarantees in medicine, but still, this is as close to one as we've ever hoped for, and while it may sound cold, for every soldier you heal, there are more resources for those you can't help. Some of those VA hospitals find themselves stretched pretty thin at times. Cutting down on their patient load will definitely help them cope."

"Glad to hear it, Doctor, glad to hear it." Steve got out his card and passed it over. "Please have your people call my office so we can set up a schedule to get everyone taken care of."

Doctor Carella smiled again. "Thanks again. I have to say while all these changes we're going through are a little worrisome at times, it's nice to see there's an upside to all of it. We've got thousands of disabled veterans around the greater DC area alone."

"Thousands, you say?" Tisha asked.

"Oh, yes, the number of disabled vets is a lot higher than many people realize, because most of them don't talk about it."

"Interesting," she said with a smile. "Now if you'll forgive us?"

"Oh, of course! Have a good day!"

Steve walked off with Tisha as the doctor pocketed his card.

"I can hear the gears turning, Tisha," Steve said.

"Well, I am thinking. What are we going to do with all these experienced veterans once they've been infected?"

"Part of that will depend on them, part of it will depend on what they're doing now, and part of it will depend on what I decide."

"Only part?" Tisha laughed.

"Okay, a big part," Steve admitted. "As much as I'm sure there are a lot of people who'd want to send them to the front, I think it might be time to start up some sort of 'home guard' for the DC area. This city is a target, and a big one. We put them in a reserve unit or something like that, and have them on duty once or twice a week."

"Sounds reasonable."

"Yeah, and I'll need some bodies to replace all the people I'll be drafting to start the new shop here," Steve added with a grin.

"Better hope Sean doesn't find out!"

"Oh, I don't think he wants a job here, so I'm not worried. Now, let's gather up our minders and head over to see Kensington."

"What do we need to see him for?"

"I promised Sean I'd see if I couldn't get him to lean on the FBI to go after the west coast ALS folks."

"They're still a problem?" Tisha asked, a little surprised.

"I think Sean's worried they might become one again. They've caused him trouble twice now, and I honestly think he wants them all dead at this point."

"Sounds like the First is rubbing off on him."

Steve nodded and then sighed after a moment. "We've changed. All of us. We've changed a lot more than I think any of us ever expected. All I ever wanted was to have a chain of auto repair stores across the country."

"And now?" Tisha asked.

"Now I want to run it. I see all these idiots doing stupid shit, ruining people's lives, and not paying attention, and I *know* I can do better."

Tisha laughed. "I've heard that song sung before."

"Yeah, but I have something the others didn't have."

"Oh?"

"I have Sean to keep me honest. He's my best friend; there's no way he'll let me mess it all up."

#

Sean sat down in his makeshift workshop. Things here were still a mess, and he had no idea when he'd be able to clean it all up. He thought about his workshop in the basement of the building he owned in Sparks; maybe he could use that one for now? At least it wasn't a mess.

He'd given Estrella her collar back; he hadn't been able to combine the lycan collar enchantments with it, he just didn't have the time right now to figure out the best way to do it. It was one of those things that would definitely be a major undertaking. He had tarred it, figuring he could make a couple of copies, but the amount of energy that would take was somewhere on the order of 'stupendous'. It was an order of magnitude harder than even the silver tag.

He'd wondered about that at first, but the truth was, his father's spell was in some ways simpler than one making someone appear to disappear.

Plus his father's tag was made by a genius, plain and simple. The invisibility enchantment on the collar was just the reworking of an existing series of spells. The enchanter who had created it hadn't done anything to make it more efficient. Sean suspected he was going to have to do that himself, which would mean learning the faerie method of enchanting even more thoroughly than he already had.

Again, a project for when the war was over.

He went through the memories he'd gotten from the demon lord next. There weren't many of them left; perhaps if he'd spent more time concentrating on them he'd have remembered more of them, but he'd been in the middle of combat at the time and was just a bit distracted.

What did stick out was the magic missile spell. It was one he was already interested in, and had archived a copy out of his defensive shield framework. So his mind hadn't had any problems grabbing onto that bit of knowledge.

As he'd thought before, the spell's simple appearance was deceptive. As he got farther down into it, it became more and more complicated. In some ways, it was constructed much like the way he had been using his magic—lots of 'library' type modules at the bottom that were all linked together to form the larger spell.

And that's where it got *strange*.

Because *all* of the 'library-like' structures were there; even though the majority of each library wasn't being used, it was all still there, all of it, including all sorts of interesting abilities and tricks. It was like a first-year programming student writing 'hello world' and then linking into every stinking library on the machine when they went to compile it. It was definitely overkill, and Sean could easily rewrite the spell into a much more compact, and therefore less energy consuming, format.

But...but because the spell had all these extra libraries linked into it, it inadvertently picked up a lot of little things from them. Almost like inheritance properties. Like, its ability to home in on electric fields was an error state that was accidentally linked in, and it switched to when it couldn't find any kind of life force.

It couldn't be shielded against, because it was constantly running through so many states as its 'program' ran that no shield could block against it; it just changed properties too often. Sean's had only worked because it absorbed the spell's energy instead of trying to stop it, and unlike the really nasty spells that had been thrown at him when he was retreating with Estrella that time, it wasn't powerful enough to blow his shield down by overwhelming the draining process.

Sean sat there and considered that. If he grabbed all those libraries and put them into his own 'library', he could then link them into a new shield spell. That made him wonder if could he get the same effect the magic missile had? Would the shield keep shifting its properties fast enough that any one type of attack, or perhaps even a varying attack like the missile, wouldn't be able to get through?

Could he then absorb spells like that powerful attack he'd been hit with before? And if so, what would he have to do to manage all the energy?

Then there was the 'mana shield' he'd been thinking of. If he ever went back to the blockhouse, he was going to need it; with the main gateway now open all the time, getting near it would overload him. Possibly burn him out or kill him. It might do the same to any other magic user who was with him, too. So it was going to have to be an enchantment he could place on an object, not just cast into his framework.

Pondering that question, he opened up his classroom and went inside. Bringing up his magic emulator, he loaded the missile spell into it. He'd start by pulling out all the libraries and organizing them so he could use them. Once he got that done, he'd start on the mana shield. That should be an easy task—some sort of self-powering loop to divert the energy away from the magic user. Maybe there was something in one of the new libraries he could use to burn it off by using it against itself...

When the little alarm clock spell went off, Sean leaned back, exhausted. Eight hours had gone by. *Eight* hours! He'd worked through lunch, and probably into dinner. He was a bit surprised none of the girls had come to disturb him. The mana shield had proven more difficult at first than he'd thought it would, but only because there was so much he had to learn in the new libraries. He'd had to write descriptions for each of them and document what was in them. That had taken him a lot more time than he'd realized, and there were still a few left he needed to categorize.

But he'd definitely found what he was looking for. It wasn't a shield so much as an insulator. He'd taken a lesson from the mind protection spell he'd come up with so long ago—if it couldn't touch you, it wouldn't know you were there. So the mana shield, simply put, insulated your body from all mana, powering itself off the mana it was blocking out.

Of course this led to problems with controlling it, especially once your own mana ran out, as you wouldn't be able to generate any more with the shield in place. That led to him having to install a failsafe on the program, which would allow it to be turned off with a verbal command and a gesture. Once he had that added in, he realized he could add a 'tap' to the enchantment to allow a controlled amount of mana through the shield to the user. After he'd coded that piece, he went back and redid it, giving the user the ability to adjust the flow.

The spell took more energy than he would have preferred; those extra libraries were energy hogs. Another project for after the war would be to create a new set of libraries from the old ones that were smaller and more focused.

Then he quickly built the spell up into an enchantment, and after checking it on his emulator, he tarred it up and checked his clock. Another hour had gone by! He'd look into the other shield spell later. Closing down his classroom, he opened his eyes and looked around his shop. It was late, he could tell, because it had gotten dark outside and no one had turned on a light.

He recognized a couple of werewolves from his security detail playing spades over by the door.

"Where's Cali?" Sean asked.

"Oh! Hi, Sean!" Jordan said, setting down his cards. "Roxy came and got her and left us to watch over you. She said she wanted Cali's help with checking over the new weapons."

"Didn't they tell you to wake me for dinner?"

Jordan looked a little embarrassed. "Roxy said not to bother you, and honestly? I'm not so sure I wanted to be the one to disturb you when you're in that magic trance thing."

Sean nodded slowly as he stretched. He couldn't exactly blame them.

Standing up, he went over to the door, opened it, and looked outside. There weren't a lot of lights on, but since all lycans had excellent night vision, it wasn't exactly necessary.

There were a lot of aircraft sitting out on the flight line, all their helicopters and a number of large cargo planes. Mostly C-130s but there was even a C-17 there as well!

"What's with the large cargo jet?" Sean asked as his guards got up to follow him.

"Artillery," Jordan said. "Chad ordered a bunch to be installed around here. I think if you listen hard enough you can hear him, Maitland, Roxy, Bill, Daelyn, and some arty guy arguing over where to put it."

Sean laughed at that. "Well, I'm sure they don't need me putting my two cents in. Let's go see if we can get the folks over at the mess to feed us. I'm starving!"

Territories

"We're up to six million lycans," Sean told Estrella as they lay in bed together the next morning, enjoying the afterglow of some very satisfying sex.

"Already?"

"At the rate we're going, I suspect it'll be ten million by the end of the month."

"That just seems...well, strange."

"Why's that?"

"Because all these years, dad told everyone 'no infecting'. He laid down the law on that I don't know how long ago."

"Probably when he decided he didn't want to be king of the world anymore."

"You may be right. So where are you going to open up this portal? Here?"

Sean shook his head. "I have no idea how long it'll stay open and what kind of control I'll have over it. I want to put it someplace safe."

"Put it in the dwarven town, then."

Sean shook his head. "No. I don't think I want to put it someplace where it's under someone else's control. I've been thinking our bunker."

"We have a bunker?"

Sean nodded. "It's north of here, at the south end of Reno. Just where the hills start. We may have to abandon it, though, when we pull out of Reno. Are djevels any good at finding things underground?"

"Digging isn't exactly their strong suit. Hell, just getting them to hoe a furrow in the ground was a major undertaking. Is it shielded from magic?"

Sean nodded.

"There you go. They'll never find it unless someone leads them to it."

"Well, let's go grab a car and drive up there."

"What, now?" Estrella asked, looking down at her sweaty and mussed body.

"Okay, after we shower."

"And grab a bite to eat."

"And grab a bite to eat," Sean said with a sigh.

"Who do you want to bring along?"

Sean almost said 'nobody', but after thinking about it a minute, he changed his mind.

"Jo."

"Why her?"

"Because she warded the place originally, so she can check the wards."

"Aren't you worried about finding someone else in there?"

"We keep a small squad of troops there at all times. It's one of the few safe houses we have that our core people know about."

"You know Cali and the others will be mad if you sneak out without them."

"We're messing with lion magic. I'm probably going to have everyone evacuate the place just in case something goes wrong."

"What could possibly go wrong?"

"Oh, I don't know, Mom and Dad spanking our asses?"

Estrella laughed, and then thought about it a second. "Yeah, better to evacuate everyone first. Wouldn't want anyone to see *that* happening!"

§

"Hi, Mom! Hi, Dad!" Sean said, grinning as he popped into the lion realm.

"Let me guess, you want to know what I had to do with the French attacking Berlin," the First said with a heavy sigh.

Estrella had shown up at that moment as well and was stretching a bit.

"Umm, actually, no. Why would you think that?"

"Because it's the middle of the day? Normally you only show up now if there's a problem, or if you're mad about something."

Sean considered that and nodded slowly. "Yeah, I guess that's been true more often than not of late. But that's not why we're here today."

"Oh?" the First said, looking curious.

"Buuuut, as long as you offered," Sean said with a smirk, " what *did* you have to do with the French nuking Berlin?"

"The French have gotten very paranoid about being invaded from the east, and given recent history, one can hardly blame them. We've been keeping them advised of the situation in Berlin, and we advised them that now was the best time to strike."

"So you actually *did* have a plan for this, Father?" Estrella asked.

The First nodded. "The French government is used to dealing with magic users. It didn't take a lot of effort to set up yesterday's events.

"So, why *are* the two of you here?"

Sean looked around for Keairra and waved her over.

"Well, it's like this," Sean said with a grin...

"We want you all to come back to Earth." Estrella smiled.

"What?" Keairra said walking up to them. "Even if we had enough pregnant lionesses, nine months plus at least a dozen years?" She laughed. "I don't think so."

Sean held up a hand. "I'll be right back."

The First blinked as Sean disappeared. "What is he up to?"

"Oh, you'll find out very shortly!" Estrella grinned.

Just then they all felt it, a large drain on their lion energy pool.

"He didn't!" the First said, standing up on all four feet.

"Is that a *gateway*?" Keairra said as a six-foot diameter disk suddenly formed nearby.

"Sure looks like one!" Kearu said, padding over.

"Stay away from that!" the First growled just as Sean reappeared.

"Taa-daa!" Sean said, looking around and then pointing at the gateway.

"*What did you do*?" the First growled in an ominous voice.

"I opened a portal from that underground shelter we were using to here! What do you think?" Sean said, still smiling. "This way *everyone* here can go back to Earth, and we don't have to wait for you to be reborn again!"

Keairra looked at Sean in shock. "You can do that?"

"Apparently," Sean said with a nod. "When Dad here got kicked out of my head, my stats spell locked onto all the abilities he'd left in my head, I guess. Or maybe it was there all the time and I just missed it? In either case, opening up the gateway takes a *lot* of power."

"That was what we felt!" Howart said, padding around the gateway.

"Yeah. Apparently it's the same ability we use to project here, but it costs a hell of a lot more to open an actual *physical* gate."

Sean noticed then that the First was still growling, if only softly.

"What's wrong, Father?" Sean asked, coming over and dropping to his knees in front of the First to put his head on the same level.

"Why didn't you ask me about this?"

"Did you know I could do it?" Sean asked.

"Actually, no, I didn't."

"Because you would have told me not to, and then we would have had a big fight when I did it anyway," Sean admitted.

"Oh, we're still going to have a big fight."

"Why?"

"Because we're dead! We can't go through that thing!"

"How do you know?"

"Because nothing is ever that simple!" the First said with a loud growl.

"Well, maybe this is!" Sean growled back. "Besides, this was hardly *simple*!"

"*Sean*!"

"I did this because I *need* you, Dad. Not here, but on Earth, with the rest of us! Because I need everybody here! I'm tired of doing all this by myself! Just me! This is the big fight, the fight that will determine the fate of the world, and *dammit*! I want you with me! Not sitting up here!"

"Sean..."

"I'll check it out."

Sean and the First looked to find Sampson was standing by the gate.

"No! I forbid it!" the First growled.

"Uh-huh. Right, *grandfather*!" Sampson laughed and made a rude gesture. "Like I'm going to start listening to you all of a sudden after all these years!"

With that, Sampson stepped through.

And disappeared.

"Is he?" someone muttered.

"He doesn't feel dead," Keairra muttered.

Several seconds went by, then Sampson came back out. "Well? What are you waiting for?"

"It works?" Howart asked.

"Course it works!"

Sampson turned and went back through, with Howart hot on his heals.

"Don't everyone rush!" Estrella called. "It's not a big room, and we'll have to figure out where to put everybody!"

"Sean..." the First started, his voice a cross between a growl and an exasperated sigh.

Keairra put her hand on the First's head, stopping him. "Leave it, Dear."

"But!"

"I said, leave it. Our son loves us and wants us with him. You should be proud he figured this out."

The First blinked. "You don't expect..." he said looking bewildered.

Sean's eyes were open wide as he looked from the First to Keairra and back again.

"Course I do. Now get up. We're going through."

"But..."

"Dad!" Estrella growled. "You can either walk through, or we'll drag you!"

The First looked at Sean. "You, young man, are in trouble. We *will* be having words!"

Sean watched as the First went over to the gateway. "Come through a hundred at a time, with a half hour break between groups!" the First said, looking around the hillside.

"Who's going?" Kearu asked.

"I'd like ten volunteers to stay for now. Otherwise, everybody." The First looked at Sean, and then Estrella. "You two might as well wake up."

§

Waking up, Sean opened his eyes and sat up just as the First walked through the gateway. Sampson was already standing there, and Sean couldn't help himself; getting to his feet, he threw himself at Sampson and hugged him.

"Sampson! I can't believe you're alive again! Well, okay I can believe it! But it's so great to have you back! Oh, god, how I've missed you! I know Mom's missed you too! And everything that's happened and the whole world's gone crazy and..."

"Sean!" Sampson interjected.

"Yes?"

"You're babbling, and yeah, dying sucked but," Sampson laughed, "it is great to be back! And without having to grow up all over again, too!"

Sean gave him another hug and then all but charged the First and nearly bowled him over as he threw his arms around his neck. Estrella was already tangled up with Keairra.

"Dad! It's so great to have you here!"

The First sighed. "You've been seeing me constantly."

"But it's not the same! You're alive again!"

"It has been a while, but when you've been around as long as I have, it's not all that different really, Son."

Sean laughed. "Yeah, but now I can hit you and you'll actually feel it!"

"We better move out of the way," Sampson said. "This room is going to fill up rather fast. Where are we, anyway?"

"The machine room for an old fallout shelter the dwarves built for some friends. Let's head upstairs, and I'll tell the local werewolves what to expect."

"What are we going to do about the gate?" Keairra asked.

"I'm certain I can collapse it once everyone is out, and reopening it shouldn't cost me as much the second time around. From what I've seen of these abilities, it's the initial establishment of the gate that sucks up all the energy. After that, I'm hoping it's much cheaper to use," Sean said as he led everyone up the stairs. "But for now, I think I'll just leave it up."

"First, you know where everything is here, give me a moment to run up to the garage and let everyone know it's safe to come back in."

"Why are they all up there?" the First asked.

"Because I thought it would be safer."

"You didn't know what was going to happen?" the First grumbled, eyes narrowing as he looked at Sean.

"Well, *you* didn't know what would happen, and you've been doing this mystical shit a lot longer than I have!" Sean said with a smile.

The First watched as Sean went up the stairway to the garage above. Estrella was off talking to one of her friends; Sampson was watching him and Keairra, who was standing beside him.

"Notice anything?" she asked him.

"I notice a lot of things," the First replied.

"I feel a lot stronger than the last time I was alive."

The First ducked his head in a nod. "There are more lycans alive now than there have been in a *very* long time."

"How many are you going to let them make?" Sampson asked.

"Until this war is over, as many as they want."

"We'll end up with problems," Keairra warned.

"Then we'll deal with those problems," the First said. "But think about it, even if only half of one percent of the population becomes lycans, that's still over thirty million."

"Aren't you worried about trouble?" Sampson asked.

The First snorted. "There will always be trouble, Sampson. It is the nature of life for there to be trouble. But I think enough of us have learned our lessons that *we* won't be the ones starting it this time." The First looked around a moment, thoughtful. "It's going to take days to move everyone out of our world back here. I guess I'll have to talk to someone about setting up a ferry. Maybe Oak."

Sampson suddenly laughed.

"What?"

"If you try to take over your son's job, you know he's going to beat you to death."

"Oh, I don't think he's that strong yet."

"He will be if I'm holding you down!"

The First looked at Sampson challengingly. "Think you can, *Grandson*?"

"I'll be helping him, dear!" Keairra laughed.

"I should have known better than to let the two of you come out together," the First grumbled with a shake of his head.

"Don't worry, Dear. We'll still let you pretend to be in charge!" Keairra teased. "Ah, here he comes!"

They watched as Sean came down the stairs with Jolene.

"Jo, this is the First, whom you recall used to live in my head."

"Hi, Dad," Jolene said and dropped to her knees to give him a hug.

"And now that you're not in my head anymore, she's hands off; same for the rest of my wives," Sean said with a slight growl.

The First smiled and hugged Jolene back with a massive paw. "It's nice to see you again, Jo, as unexpected as it is." He glanced up at Sean. "Of course. Though with Keairra and *my* pride around, straying isn't something I do."

"Cause we don't let him," Keairra said with a grin.

"Jo, this is Keairra, and I believe you've met Sampson?"

"Hello, Keairra," Jolene said, rising back up and giving her a hug. She then turned to Sampson and shook hands. "Actually, I've never had the pleasure."

Sean made a few more introductions, and then introduced the wolf who was currently in charge of the bunker.

"This is Rider, he's the one in charge this week. We rotate some of our more experienced people through here on a regular schedule. This place is still secret, so only about two hundred lycans know where it is now."

"Great. Pele!" the First called to one of the lions.

"Yes?"

"You can stay here for now and help. Work with Rider here and make sure everyone here knows they can't talk to *anyone* about the gateway. Ever. Not even to each other, just one of us lions."

"Got it!"

"Now, if it's all the same, to you, Son, I'd really like to go outside and take a look at the place. I haven't been here, in the flesh, in a *very* long time."

"Of course!" Sean said, and led them all up the stairs and out of the bunker.

"We're going to need a couple of buses or something," Jolene mused.

Sean nodded. "I told Rider to call for transport when I led everyone back inside."

"You know there are going to be a lot of very shocked people when you show up with a hundred lions," Jolene pointed out.

"Just wait until they see the other twenty thousand of them," Sean said with a sudden realization.

"And what are you going to do with Sampson?"

"Huh?"

"Roberta and he used to be an item?" Jolene said, prompting him.

"Actually, we um, sort of had this discussion a while ago. Rob's mine now. They're exes."

"Sarah might not understand that."

"Sarah *is* his daughter. Don't worry, I'm sure we'll work it out," Sean told her.

"Oh, you brought the van," the First said. "Why don't the six of us head back to your new place?"

"Six?" Sean asked.

"You, me, Esti, Jo, Key, and Sampson. Howart and the others can either wait for ground transport or get there on foot."

"It's thirty miles," Jolene warned.

"Just make sure to stay out of the way of traffic!" Estrella said, turning around to the group of lions who had followed them upstairs. "The people around here drive like maniacs!"

Sean had to laugh at that. "How long has it been since these folks have been alive?"

"For some, centuries," Keairra said. "Then for certain others, like say your dad there, a couple millennia."

Sean looked at the First, who shrugged as he padded along beside them on all fours. "I like it in our little world. Now, someone get the door for me and let's go."

Shock to the System

Someone had asked Rider if they could borrow the other van that was used to ferry people and goods into the bunker, so Rider had supplied a driver, and when Sean parked by the new buildings that had been set up for them, another dozen lions got out along with Sean and his group.

To say people stopped and stared would be very accurate.

"You know what?" Sean said, looking around. "I just realized I now have twenty thousand people I have to find places to live, feed, and outfit."

"Don't worry, most of them won't be staying here," the First said.

"What?"

"Almost half will be sent to South America to help down there, and at least a quarter of them I'm going to send to Europe to help Raban."

"That's still a lot to coordinate," Sean said, looking around.

"They're adults, they can handle it themselves," the First said with a dismissive gesture of his paw. "Now, let's go inside. You can introduce us and see if you can talk the twins into making lunch."

"Hungry already?"

"Actually, I need to go down for a nap soon, seeing as I just left everybody without any real orders," the First said with an embarrassed look.

"You did just blindside him, you know," Keairra added.

Sean gave an embarrassed look of his own. "I guess I sorta got carried away in the heat of the moment. But we both know if I'd warned him, he would have found an excuse to say no."

"He's right, Mom," Estrella said. "Everyone says Dad is nothing if not fond of sitting on his mountain all day and telling the rest of us how to live."

The First just shook his head as Keairra chuckled and hip checked him. "They're on to you, Dear."

Sean opened the door and led them inside to the area his wives had claimed as their living space. The second they set foot inside, Sarah streaked by, yelling "Daddy!" and latched onto Sampson's leg.

"Daddy! You're back! You're back! They told me you'd gone away!"

Sean watched as Sampson kneeled down and gave his daughter a hug.

"Yes, well your other daddy, Sean, did something special so I could come back and see you."

"Sampson?"

Sean looked up, and Roberta was standing there looking very shocked, and obviously a little conflicted as well. Sean took two large steps and, standing beside her, he put an arm around her. Sampson looked up and sighed, but then smiled.

"Yes, it's me. Sean opened a gate into the lion world, and we're coming back, all of us. Umm, I know he's your husband now, and I'm okay with it. I *was* dead, after all."

Roberta looked at Sean and smiled. "Yes, I'm married. But can I at least give you a hug? I missed you, Sam, I missed you a lot." Roberta gave Sean a hug. "Don't growl, Hon, he may have been my first, but *you're* my one and only now."

Sean blushed; he hadn't even realized he'd been growling.

"Sorry, Sampson."

"Don't be," Sampson said with a shrug, looking up from Sarah, whom he'd picked up. "It happens."

Roberta freed herself from Sean's arm, walked over and gave Sampson a big hug, and smiled up at him. "Thanks for biting him. Sean told me you really didn't want to do it, but events forced your hand."

Sampson looked a little sad. "Yeah, they did. But I guess it all turned out alright."

Roberta laughed. "Oh, *did they*! Hate to diss you, Sam, but, well..."

"You prefer Sean."

Roberta nodded and gave him another hug, then looked at Sarah. "Your daughter, however, may have other feelings," she said with a giggle.

Sampson smiled at that, and Roberta walked back over to Sean and gave him a kiss. Sean suddenly felt a lot better about things.

"Well, now that Rob has defused that situation," Roxy said, looking down at the First, "you just gonna go native all day, or do you think you could do the polite thing and go on two legs for a while?"

Keairra laughed at that, and with a sigh the First shifted into his hybrid form.

"Damn, he really is big, isn't he?" Daelyn said, walking up next to Roxy. The First was at least a foot taller than Sean, who was eight-foot-tall in his hybrid form.

"You need higher ceilings," the First noted, as his ears were now brushing up against it.

"Everyone, this is Keairra, the First's mate, and also the next in charge after him," Sean told them. "Keairra, this is Roxy, Daelyn, Peg, Cali, Roberta, and of course you already met Jolene, and I think you still remember your daughter's name?"

Keairra smiled and gave each of the girls a hug.

"I find it interesting that you have the same number of wives as your father," Keairra said with a glance at the First.

"You have seven wives, First?" Roxy asked, looking at him.

"The others haven't come through yet. I suspect they're riding herd on everyone as they come," the First said.

"Come through?" Roxy asked, looking at Sean. "What has he done this time, and what do I need to do to him for doing it?"

Sean heard both the First and Keairra snicker at that.

Sean shrugged. "Oh, I just figured out how to open a gate to the lion la-la land and get everyone out of it."

"How many is 'everybody'?"

"A bit more than twenty thousand?" Sean said, trying to look innocent, and failing miserably.

"Twenty *thousand*?" Roxy asked incredulously.

Sean nodded.

"Lions?" Daelyn asked.

Sean nodded again.

"Why do I feel like rubbing my hands together like Flounder and saying, 'This is gonna be great'?" Daelyn asked, looking at Roxy with a gleeful look.

"Umm, because it is?" Roxy said with a sudden grin. "But we better go find Oak before he has a heart attack!"

"Could someone find me a place where I can rest undisturbed for a while?" the First asked.

"Just grab a corner," Roxy said. "If you have a pride coming, I'm going to have to find someplace special, a nice room for all of you. Peg, could you please tell Dania and Rania that we have some unexpected guests and to fetch over a bunch of food from the mess?"

"Oh it!"

"Thanks! Come on, Dae, let's get cracking."

"Reminds me of you," the First said, looking over at Keairra. "Let me know when food gets here." With that he shifted back into a lion, curled up by the end of the couch, and dropped off to sleep.

Sean looked over at Sampson, who was still entertaining Sarah.

"Sarah, can I borrow him for a while?"

"But he just got here!"

"And he's going to be here from now on. But there are some other people who would like to see your father again, and it wouldn't be fair to them to wait, now would it?"

"Ummm," Sarah said, looking back and forth, a little confused.

"Sarah," Roberta called. "Sampson has things to do. Don't worry, he'll be back!"

"O-kay, Mom," Sarah said in a sulky voice.

"Don't worry, I'll be back," Sampson said in a voice a lot more cheerful and soft than Sean ever recalled hearing Sampson use before as he set her down.

"Thanks, Sarah," Sean said. Grabbing Sampson's arm, he lead him out of the room and down the hallway.

"I can walk, Sean," Sampson growled.

Sean laughed. "Yup, and so can I. Besides, I don't want you getting cold feet, Dad."

"I thought the First was dad now?"

"You both are. So is Roxy's dad. But I thought it might be confusing." Sean stopped in front of a door and knocked on it. He could hear someone putting stuff away and organizing the room.

"One minute!" Sean's mother's voice came from the other side of the door.

Sean felt Sampson freeze.

"You try to run off on me and I will magic your ass, Dad." Sean grinned.

Louise opened the door then and saw two very large lion weres. One she knew was her son Sean, and the other she also recognized instantly.

"Sampson?" she said, eyes wide.

Sampson smiled, a little weakly. "Hi, Lou."

"But, but I thought you were dead?"

"We don't die; I thought your son told you that?"

Louise looked at Sean.

"We go to a sort of afterlife, a special place for lions. While we wait to reincarnate. Turns out there are ways to leave early."

"Oh!" Louise said, and then to Sampson's surprise , she threw herself at him and wrapped her arms around him, hugging him, and even gave him a kiss.

For his part, Sampson hugged her back, feeling just a little awkward. He really did love her, but...but she'd been his best friend's wife, after all. Looking over at Sean, he noticed Sean had a big shit-eating grin on his face, and he suddenly recalled what Sean had said to him almost two years ago.

"Mom, Dad?" Sean said and putting his hands on Sampson's back, he pushed them both into Louise's room.

They both looked at him and blinked.

"Siblings. I want siblings. Don't either one of you come out until I've got one on the way, got it?"

"But..." Sampson started.

"No excuses!" Sean looked at his mother, who'd started to open her mouth as well.

"Mom! Can it. I spent the last decade watching the two of you dance around this. Well, no more. Now go make me a little sister or something!" Sean said. Stepping out of the room, he adroitly closed the door.

"I think we've been set up," Sampson growled.

Louise laughed. "I think you're right. But do you really think he went through all this trouble just to hook us up?"

"This *is* Sean we're talking about," Sampson grumbled. "So, yeah. I do."

"You know, I just cleaned off the bed, maybe we should have this discussion over there?"

Sampson looked down at her. "Is this what you want?"

"Yes, it's what I want. Very much...don't you?"

Sampson gave a lustful growl. "More than you can imagine."

"Where's Sampson?" Roberta asked when Sean came back.

"Making me a little sister, I hope!" Sean snickered.

"You didn't!" Jolene said, laughing.

"Actually, if he hadn't, I was going to suggest it," Roberta said, smirking. "Sampson always wore his heart on his sleeve, and I *know* he's always had a thing for Louise."

"And my mom has a thing for him," Sean said. "I think she was always worried about what I'd think if she took up with someone else. Well, I'm 'out of the house now', as they say. Besides which, now I won't be paranoid whenever he's around Rob."

"Good point," Jo agreed. "So what's next on your schedule?"

"Talk to dad over there when he wakes up and see about putting together three teams to go through a small portal one of these cycles."

"That's the real reason you opened that gateway, isn't it?" Keairra asked from where she was sitting on the couch by the First's sleeping form.

Sean nodded. "I figured if I could open one from here, then if worse comes to worse, I can open one from there, and we can all escape back into our own world and not end up trapped like Stell was."

"And dragging both Sampson and the First back?"

"Was just icing on the cake." Sean winked at her and then grinned. "I love it when a plan comes together!"

"Why do I have the sudden urge to throttle him?" Keairra asked Estrella.

"Because he's quoting some obscure modern culture reference," Estrella replied. "I'm still getting used to it."

"The A-Team is not obscure!" Sean protested.

"Our husband, the dork," Jolene said with a smile.

"Well, if you'll both excuse me, I have to go round up twenty thousand lycan collars and silver tags for all the new guests."

"Aren't all the machines in Vegas now?"

"Almost all. There are still a couple down in Dae's home in the local dwarven halls, but that's why I've got to go make arrangements. I think we only have a thousand in stock here, but with all the recruits we have coming through, I'm not even sure about that."

"Not having to worry about one's clothes being destroyed is definitely something I would love to experience," Keairra said with a pleased expression. "So by all means, go find us some collars, Sean."

"I think you've been dismissed, Husband!" Cali laughed.

"Apparently. I'll see you all around dinner," Sean said with a wave and went outside to get started. He definitely had a lot to do, but first he'd check on the stocks of collars and tags. Back at the ranch, they'd always kept a couple thousand handy because of all the recruiting that'd been going on. Then he'd call the group managing the machines in Vegas and put in one hell of an order.

After that, he'd call a meeting and bring everyone up to date on the situation.

#

Betty was sitting in the new mess by herself. The guys were all still back at the barracks at the 'Ranch', but they'd evacuated all the civilians, support, and non-essential personnel the other night, and that had included her.

She wasn't exactly happy about that, and neither was her boyfriend Josh, or any of the other Marines she'd been staying with, but the order had been given, and as she was still human; they weren't going to be making any exceptions.

She was bunking with Elliana, Steff, Julia, and Kate again. Stewart had rescued the four girls from some sort of cult that made the one she'd been in look like kindergarten. Betty wasn't up on all the details, but they still called Stewart 'The Voice', and would do whatever he said without hesitation.

The fact that he wasn't screwing them, when they all obviously wanted him, impressed the hell out of Betty. Those girls were hot, and she'd never met a man with that kind of restraint before—not one as young as Stewart, at least. The four of them went around like cats in heat, and she'd be shocked if they were sleeping alone come tomorrow night.

Of course the first month she'd been here, she hadn't been all that different. She'd gone a little crazy, and pretty much had been bed hopping like a bunny. When she'd found the Marines—or perhaps it would be better to say they'd found her—she'd quickly narrowed her own focus until she'd ended up sleeping with Josh, and only Josh. He was older than her, but not too much older, wiser, more experienced, and the kind of guy no one liked to mess with. He'd even been teaching her how to shoot, use a knife, and anything else handy if she had to defend herself.

Her head came up then as the mess went dead silent. Looking around, she saw a lion enter the room. It wasn't Sean or Adam; she knew what both of them looked like now.

Then another lion entered right behind him, and another, then a string of lionesses who were all chatting with each other. As she watched, they trooped over to the chow line and made their way through it, teasing the stunned servers who quickly got their wits back, and then headed for the tables.

Elliana, Steff, Julia, and Kate immediately waved at the lions, flagging them over to their table, already whispering to each other about *finally* having a shot at one. Betty cringed a little; she knew lions were like kings, and you had to do what they said. But she really had no interest in getting comfy with anyone other than Josh anymore.

"This seat taken?" a lioness asked, looking down at her.

Betty shook her head.

"Great! Julia and Shin! I found a spot!"

Betty blinked as two other lionesses came over and sat on the other side of her.

"I'm Umnsalo, or just Uma for short," the lioness said, sitting down. "You had that 'deer in the headlights' look when the 'four temptresses' over there flagged the boys down, so I figured maybe you'd could use a little insulation."

"I'm Betty. You know about them?"

"Course I do; what one lion knows..."

"We all know!" Julia and Shin said with a chuckle from their seats.

"And trust me," Uma continued, "we all heard about those four when Sean's student took them in. I think the boys are definitely going to be keeping them occupied for a while. So what's your story?"

"Don't you know?"

"Wouldn't be asking if I did. You're obviously human, attractive, and you're not looking for anybody, which leads me to guess you already have a man?"

Betty nodded. "Josh, he's a Marine, and he's still up at the ranch."

"She's that kid the preacher shot," Shin said and then stopped to give her a pat on the leg. "Sorry to hear about that, must have been rough."

Betty blinked again. "Umm, I think I'm over it. Well, except for what happened to my father."

All three of the lionesses nodded. "He did it for you, you know."

"No, I don't know," Betty whispered, looking down.

"Well, you do now," Uma said. "He redeemed himself, and you should remember him for that; he obviously loved you very much. So, thinking about becoming a lycan?"

Betty's head came back up at the sudden change in topic. She looked at Uma, who was focused on eating her dinner.

"A lycan, are you thinking of becoming one?" Uma asked again between bites. "If your boyfriend is one, well, I'd think you'd be considering it too. All the Marines are jaguars, right?"

"Josh is, but some of them are tigers or bears and stuff."

"So thinking about it?"

Betty blushed. "Well, yeah, I have been. You're all so strong and tough and self-assured," Betty's voice lowered. "Something I'm not, really."

"You came up to Sean's place and got yourself a Marine boyfriend. Sounds pretty self-assured to me," Shin teased.

"I didn't have anywhere else to go!" Betty protested.

"So you went straight into the arms of the devil after getting shot?" Shin winked. "Sounds like you started thinking for yourself and decided to find out the truth."

"I wanted security," Betty said and blushed again. "I wanted to be safe."

"If you wanted *safe*, you would have gone back to Los Angeles," Uma said. "You were looking for something more than safety, and it sounds like Josh is it, right?"

Betty thought about Josh then and smiled.

"Yup, she's hot for Josh alright," Julia said, glancing over at Betty, causing her to blush yet again.

"So, the rules are pretty simple," Uma said. "If you want to have kids with Josh, you have to be a jaguar like he is."

"So I should let him bite me?" Betty asked.

"Ugh! Then you'll look like his sister!"

"What?"

"You tend to look like whoever infected you. Tell you what, as soon as we're done eating, let's go check out all the jaguars here and see if we can't find a nice, hot one so you'll have a little surprise for your Josh when he gets back."

"She's already hot," Julia pointed out.

"Well then, she'll be even hotter!" Uma said with a snicker.

"But I haven't made up my mind yet!" Betty protested weakly.

"Yes you have, you just won't admit it yet."

"And how do you know that?"

"Because you're still sitting here and haven't run away."

Betty looked down at her feet, embarrassed. Because it was true. Now that she knew she couldn't have a family with Josh unless she was a jaguar like him, she wanted it. She wanted a future with him, and from the things he'd been saying lately, she knew he wanted one with her, too.

"Okay, let's go!" Uma said a few minutes later, standing up. Looking around the mess she raised her voice, "Hey! If I wanted to find a really hot looking jag fem, where would I go?"

"Sean and Claudia's casino!" a couple of the guys called back.

"That's in Reno!" Betty said. "I don't have a car!"

"Which one of you is driving?" Uma asked.

"What's in it for me?" one of the men asked.

"A fun time with three lionesses?" Shin replied with a grin.

"Well, Dad always said I'd die young," the man said and stood up. "I'm Doug. Let's go."

"Don't worry, Doug. We promise to go easy on you!"

"Where's the fun in that?" Doug asked with a grin as they followed him out the door.

#

Sean took his seat at the head of the conference table and looked around the room. They were still setting up the displays they'd used in the old one back at the ranch. While Sean might be willing to stage the helicopters out of there for their current sorties, he wasn't going to leave *his* command post so close to the front lines.

Just about everyone had shown up for this unscheduled meeting. Sean suspected the several hundred lions now wandering around the installation had something to do with that.

"Alright, so as you've probably noticed, there are a few more lions walking around outside this afternoon than there were this morning."

"I'd hardly call a hundred 'a few'," Claudia grumbled.

Sean smiled. "Well as there are going to be a lot more coming through, I think you'll consider this to be 'a few' by the time this little exercise is over."

"How many are we expecting?" Maitland asked.

"Just about all of them," Sean said. "That is, all the ones who aren't already here."

"I take it that's a lot?"

Sean nodded.

"Um, how will that affect command, and our units? Will you still be in charge?"

"I'll still be in charge. Most of the lions are only going to be passing through here to other assignments. Those who stay will either be answering to me, or they won't be dealing with anyone here but me."

"So in short," Adam said, speaking up, "nothing here is really going to change, other than we're going to end up with a few more lions to help with the fight."

"So they all came back, didn't they?" Vincent Powers, the liaison to the magic user's councils, asked.

"Yes," Sean said looking over at him. "The lions have all returned. Well, not all, but most. I've been discussing this with the one in charge, and he agreed to my requests for help, as well as some of the others he's been getting."

"So what does this mean for the immediate future?" Bill asked.

"Well, I think we're going to need to borrow some of those Air Guard C130s for airlift. A number of them are going to South American and Europe. So we'll need transport. It might help if we can fly them from here to some of the major airports that are still functioning. I'm getting collars and tags for all of them as they come through, and I suspect we're going to be supplying either firearms or swords for a fair number of them, at the very least the ones who'll be staying here to help us out.

Probably have to make armor for a lot of them, too."

Sean turned towards Major Harper and Major Vanderberg, his two supply heads. "We're going to need a lot of weapons to outfit all the lions coming through. I suspect they'll be better served if they show up, wherever they're sent, armed. So if we can swing it, I'm going to need battle rifles, sidearms, and of course ammunition for them."

Major Joyce Vanderberg nodded, making notes on the pad before her. "Sure thing, Sean. How many are we talking?"

"Probably twenty-five thousand."

Sean noticed that the room got quiet enough you could hear the air conditioner blowing.

"Did you say twenty-five *thousand*?"

Sean smiled., "Could be more, could be less. But that's a good number to start with."

"How many lions are there, anyway?" Vincent asked.

"A lot more than twenty-five thousand," Adam said with a snicker.

Sean nodded slowly. He knew no one really wanted the number of lions known, and there really were a lot more than that.

"We're also going to need to clothe them. So set us up with whatever you can get your hands on. I suspect a lot of them will probably just run into town or Reno and buy what they need."

"Will we need to give them money?" Deidre asked.

Sean shrugged. "I don't know, maybe? I'll have to ask."

"Well, let me know so I can set up a cash draw for them."

"You got it," Sean agreed.

"Where are they all coming from?" Vincent asked.

"I'm not at liberty to share that information," Sean said, looking over at Vincent. "Or anything at all related to it."

"You know Arthur is going to go crazy over this, same for Joseph."

Sean chuckled. "Yeah, I'm sure they are. If we have the opportunity, I'll see if I can't schedule a meeting."

"How soon do you think I can get my hands on a bunch to use for Reno's defense?" Chad asked.

"I think that'll depend on how fast we can get them geared up and trained on the weapons. I'll have to talk to a few people, but hopefully I can get a couple hundred for you in a few days."

"Just remember," Adam warned, "they're lions, not soldiers. So warn the officers and the NCOs you put 'em with not to mouth off to them, or they'll be regretting it."

"I'll be sure to warn them," Chad said with a nod. "Just as long as they understand that I don't want *them* causing problems in the ranks. It's going to be bad enough that I've got all these 'gods' walking around everywhere. I'll probably have to put them in their own separate units."

"That's a good point," Sean said, thinking about the effect all these lions were going to have on his combat troops. He was already seeing some of those effects here at his base. "Guess I'll have to warn everyone to be on their best behavior until the troops get used to them."

Sean looked around the room. "If there's nothing else, I guess we'll call it a day until tomorrow's normal brief. Dismissed."

Sean sat back in the chair and watched as everyone got up and left, except for Chad, Maitland, and Adam, who all came over and sat with him, Roxy, Daelyn, and Cali, who had also stayed.

"Does this mean you're going ahead with your plan to go through a gateway?" Chad asked once the others had left the room.

Sean nodded. "This was the first step. Now I have to browbeat someone into agreeing with me."

"I take it that's the head lion?"

Sean nodded, and then smiled. "But I have a secret weapon."

"Oh?"

"He's my father-in-law."

"Umm, I'm not so sure that's the kind of thing you can count on."

Adam chuckled. "Sean's been calling him 'Dad' for ages now. Trust me; he has a weak spot for him."

"Does that mean he's your father too?" Chad asked.

"Nope. Estrella and I have the same mother, different fathers."

"Really?" Chad asked, looking surprised.

"Well, when you live forever, sometimes things get complicated. I wouldn't worry about it."

"Good, cause I got enough problems of my own already. That djevel army looks like it's going to start driving south here in the next day or two."

"Well, we're in a new gate cycle now, so I don't think we'll be looking to push out anytime soon. How long do you think we can hold the ranch?"

"We'll have to see how this push goes. A week? Two? Hard to say, Sean, until I see what they're willing to commit. Once we have everyone out of there, I'm not going to be making any stands to hold the place; I'll just be trying to slow them down on their drive to Reno to give our engineers as much time to fortify it as possible."

Sean nodded. "Sounds good to me. Now let's go find our guests and get some dinner."

Home Front

The First sat up as Sean and the others walked into the room, Keairra standing beside him; Sean noticed the First really did prefer his lion form. Keairra was in her hybrid form, however, as well as the six other lionesses, who were now all seated around the room.

"Everyone," the First said with a bit of a purr, "allow me to introduce my wives you haven't met yet." Pointing with his paw, he went clockwise around the room. "Saf'kij, Jipouet, Peym, Nibisa, Dienna, and Sasha."

Each of the lionesses gave a short nod as the First said their names. Sean had met Nibisa, Sasha, and Peym before, but not the other three, though he'd seen them around. There really were a lot of lions Sean had never met. Another task for another time, he guessed.

"When's dinner?" Peym asked.

"Hungry already?" the First asked.

"I haven't eaten in a couple hundred years, so yeah!" Peym said with a laugh.

"It's nice to meet you all," Roxy said with a smile. "Dinner is now. Then I'll show you where your room is. Oak's still getting it cleaned up, but it should be ready by the time we're all done eating."

"Sounds good!"

Sean followed Roxy out the door, with the First and the rest of his pride behind them. Daelyn and the rest of his wives were mingling with them, saying hello, and getting to know them. When they got to the mess hall, the First looked around.

"This is pretty big. Does everyone eat here?"

"Nah, there's not enough room for everyone in here," Roxy told him. "We've got two other mess halls; one's on the other side of the runways. For the most part we let people pick where they want to eat, but eventually we'll have to put people on a schedule."

"Once we pull out of Reno," Sean said, picking up the conversation, "we'll have way too many soldiers here for just three mess halls. I've got a couple of dwarves who are masters of logistics working on the problem."

"How about defenses?" Keairra asked.

"Chad and Maitland worked it all out. We're actually pulling a bunch of the stuff we had dug in at the ranch and moving it out here, and we've ordered a lot more from the military. Sawyer's been making himself invaluable as well; he's been hooking us up with a lot of stuff the supply heads we got from the military seem to be having problems with."

"Oh? What can he get that the military can't?"

"Poison gas, napalm, land mines, and cluster bombs with the kind of stuff that's supposed to be banned. He's also been finding us all sorts of stuff on the black market, like a number of top-secret stealth drones that someone stole."

"Oh? Where'd he get those?" the First asked.

"I don't ask," Sean said with a smile. "Sawyer is Sawyer. If I need something, he gets it, and I'm grateful. We're going to owe him a lot when this is all said and done. I think he's trying to become king of the goblins or something."

"I really would like to meet Chad and Maitland," Keairra said.

"Why's that?"

"Well, I am something of an expert on war and combat myself. It's not often I get to plan wars or defenses anymore."

Sean nodded. "I'll introduce you, you just have to remember one thing."

"That you're the boss?" Keairra said with a grin.

"No, *Chad* is the boss. He's got a solid head on his shoulders, and even Maitland is pleased with him," Sean told her as they followed Roxy over to a large table.

"He is quite good, Kea," the First said as he shifted into his hybrid form. "You'll like him."

Sean watched as they settled in. Roxy and Daelyn took Nibisa and Saf'kij up to the service line where the food was ordered, to show them how it all worked, he guessed. Everyone was talking, and he could see a certain amount of 'sorting' was going on as they all gravitated towards common interests. There were quite a few similarities between the two groups, he noticed.

When dinner was finished, he went with Roxy as she showed them where they would be staying, and then was quite surprised as Keairra, Saf'kij, Jipouet, Peym, Nibisa and Dienna physically dragged the First into the room.

"You have to understand," Sasha said with a big-ass grin as she got ready to close the door. "We don't get him alone in the real world very often."

"Does this mean we won't be seeing him in the morning?" Roxy asked with a laugh.

"I don't think you're going to be seeing him for days... Maybe even longer!" Sasha said with a wink as she closed and locked the door.

#

Betty looked around a little nervously as they walked into the casino. Uma had gotten Doug to stop at a clothing store, where the three lionesses had bought some things to wear. None of them had lycan necklaces yet, so they'd been pretty specific in their outfits. Short skirts, halters, and sandals.

In their human forms, Betty was impressed. So was Doug, who had been giving them the eye before in their hybrid forms. Now he was trying not to drool. They were sleek, with not a bit of fat on their bodies, their muscles well defined, but not at all bulky. They had well-toned legs, muscular butts, flat stomachs, and nice busts. Shin's was actually fairly generous, even by modern-day standards.

Shin and Julia were paying Doug a fair bit of attention, which was only fair, Betty figured, as they'd made him pay for their purchases. Apparently none of the lionesses had any money. Then again, they'd shown up at the mess in just their fur, so Betty wasn't all that surprised.

Betty recognized several of the men who were gambling as they came into the casino proper. They were all soldiers she'd either met or seen around at Sean's ranch.

One of them waved and came up to her. He was a werewolf, a natural one, not one who'd been bitten like her boyfriend and the other Marines.

"Hi, Betty! Who's your friend?"

"Ken, this is Uma. She's a lioness."

Betty noticed Ken stood a little straighter. "It's a pleasure to meet you, Ma'am," Ken said, giving a slight bow.

"Never met a lioness before, have you?" Uma asked with a smile.

"No, Ma'am. Just Sean, and only briefly."

"Ah, well, you can relax. We're just here to have fun."

"Still, after growing up with all the myths and legends, it's still a bit hard having them come to life."

Uma smiled sexily. "Well, maybe later we can put some of those myths to bed. Your bed that is."

Betty was surprised that Ken blushed. However, he was smiling as well, so she guessed things were good.

"So what brings you to the casino?"

"Betty here wants to be a jaguar so she can have a family with her boyfriend. It wouldn't be right to have him infect her, so I thought we'd come down here and see if we couldn't find a pretty jag fem to do the honors."

Ken opened his mouth, paused a moment, and then closed it again.

"Problem?"

"I was almost going to ask if you had permission, and then my brain caught up with my mouth," he said, looking embarrassed.

"Well, come and show us where we can find them."

Ken nodded and led them over to the bar. The waitresses, Betty noticed, were mostly walking around in their hybrid forms, but not all of them.

"They have humans working here?" Betty asked, looking around.

"Nope, not one," the woman behind the bar said. "But the health department was complaining about fur in the food and the drinks. So those of us handling food and mixing drinks stay human."

"May I ask what you are?"

"Werewolf. I'd ask why you were here, but I can see you're with a couple of lionesses, so it's probably none of my business."

"Actually," Uma said, and smiled, "we're trying to hook her up with a pretty fem jaguar so she can get infected."

"It's for my boyfriend," Betty said with a blush. "I want to give him a family."

"Well, far be it for me to be rude, and you're here with a lioness, but have you asked *him* about it?"

Betty blushed an even deeper shade of red and looked at the floor with a nod.

"Well, aren't we a brave one!" Uma said with a laugh.

The bartender shrugged. "I see people get drunk and do stupid shit all the time. I feel I've got to at least warn them."

"We've talked about it," Betty said in a soft voice. "He was going to infect me when he got his next leave."

"Ewwww," the bartender said. "Let me guess, he's not a natural lycan?"

Betty shook her head.

"And that's why we're here," Uma said.

"Yeah, shoulda known better than to question a lioness, right?" the bartender said with a grin. "Let me call the back. Ursula and Nell are on break. They're probably the best-looking jaguars in the place."

"On break?" Betty asked.

"They do an act," the bartender said and gave Betty a wink, causing her to blush all over again.

Going over to the register, she picked up the phone, dialed a number, and spoke to someone. Betty couldn't hear it over the noise in the casino.

"They'll be right out; I told them they were about to be judged by a couple of lionesses on their beauty."

"Evil," Uma said.

"Well, yeah. They work here! Now, what can I get you to drink?"

"I just hit town, so I'm broke," Uma admitted.

Betty reached into her pocket and pulled out a ten-dollar bill. "I'll have a water, but I think this should cover a drink for Uma here."

"Aww, Betty, you don't have to do that!"

"You're helping me out, and it's about the only thing I can do," Betty admitted. "I'd offer more, but I don't have a job, either."

"After you get infected, we always have openings for cocktail waitresses," the bartender supplied.

"Umm..." Betty looked around. For the most part, the job *looked* okay. "I'll think about it."

At that point two hybrid Jaguar girls came running out of the back and slid to a halt in front of the bartender, who pointed to Betty and Uma. One was black, the other was spotted, and neither one was wearing a stitch of clothing.

"You're a human, what're you doing here?" the black one asked, looking confused. She then turned to Uma. "No offense."

The spotted one rolled her eyes. "Obviously she's here to get infected. That's why she came here with a lioness. Really, Ursula, do I have to paint you a picture?"

"Well, only if it's a really sexy one!" Ursula grinned and hip checked the other one, who was obviously Nell.

"I must say, you both really are quite lovely," Uma said and gave Betty a nudge. "So, which one?"

"Umm," Betty blushed again; they really were both quite beautiful.

"Betty, Hon?" Ursula said. "You're already pretty hot as a human, so no matter who infects you, you're gonna be one well put together cat. The big things to look at are spotting patterns, eye color, ears, and tail."

"My boyfriend is with the Marines."

"Oh! Yeah, those guys are all hunks," Nell said, looking a little dreamy. "Might I suggest you let me bite you? All of them are melanistic, like Ursula here. So you don't want him looking at you and thinking about his friends, right?"

Ursula sighed. "Nell, if he's looking at her and thinking about his friends, I think she'd got bigger problems!"

Betty couldn't help it, she giggled at the two of them.

"Do you think you could do a couple of poses? Maybe turn around a couple of times?" Uma asked.

"Oh! Right!" Nell said, and the two girls did just that. By the time they were done, Betty noticed that there were a lot of men standing around them, about half of whom were in hybrid form.

"So, which one you gonna pick, Betty?" Doug asked, coming over with Shin and Julia.

"They're both so pretty, it's hard to pick! I mean, which one will my boyfriend Josh like the most? Once I pick, I can't change."

"Is he black or spotted?" someone called out.

"Black."

"Spotted!" a bunch of men called out.

"Huh?"

"Most black cats hook up with spotted," the first voice said. "Trust me!"

Betty shrugged and looked at the girls, who both nodded. "It's true," Nell said.

Betty looked at Uma next. "Hey, I'm a lioness, we're all brown."

"Tawny," Shin hissed and elbowed her. "It's 'tawny', not brown!"

Betty giggled again. "Okay, I'll go with spotted. So now what?"

Nell walked up to her and took her hand. "I can bite you on the arm, but I've been told on the leg works better."

"Yeah, it hurts less," one of the guys said. When Betty looked at him, he continued, "I'm one of the 'recruiters'. I've infected hundreds of guys."

"What about the scar?" Betty asked.

"This doesn't leave one."

"So, drop your pants and let's do it," Nell said.

"Here?"

"Sure, why not? Nudity isn't much of a taboo for lycans, and you're gonna turn into a cat not all that long after I bite you."

"Really?"

Uma nodded. "It's pretty typical. You'll shift into full cat, and probably stay like that until you go to bed. In the morning you'll wake up human. Then we can start teaching you."

Betty nodded slowly, and carefully knelt down and took off her sneakers, then her socks. Standing back up, she looked around nervously, then undid her jeans and pulled them off, leaving her in just her top and her panties.

"Okay, sit down and look the other way a moment," Nell said, dropping to her knees as Betty sat.

"Will this take...ouch!" Betty blinked and looked down; Nell's mouth was full of her thigh.

The pain of the bite was quickly replaced with a cool, tingling feeling. When Nell released her leg, it bled slowly for about a minute, and then stopped.

Betty blinked and felt a little dizzy.

"How long will this take?"

"About five minutes," the voice from the crowd said, coming up behind her.

Betty suddenly recognized the voice. Looking up, she saw it was Josh!

"What are *you* doing here?"

Josh smiled down at her. "Doug called me while you were all shopping. Told me what was going on, so I thought I'd show up to offer moral support."

"Is this your boyfriend?" Uma asked.

Betty nodded. "Josh, this is Uma. She's a lioness."

"Oh!" Josh said and bowed to her.

"She's not as bad as Sean is!" Betty giggled.

"Sean makes them bow?" Uma said, looking surprised.

"We err, kinda put our worst foot forward the first time we met him," Josh confessed. "We've since been ordered to bow, and if needs be, grovel. Our commander was *really* unhappy with us."

"I aaa, feel funny," Betty said, giving her head a shake.

"We better get you out of that blouse and the rest of your things before you ruin 'em," Josh said, and moving around in front of her, helped her pull her top off. Betty shifted into a jaguar just as it cleared her head.

"You gals want to come up to the ranch and check it out?" Josh asked, looking at the lionesses. "I'll take Betty out for a run, and she can stay with me until morning."

"Didn't they just evacuate her?"

"They evacuated all the *humans*," Josh said with a grin. "Lycan civilians don't have to leave until tomorrow night."

"Oh, well in that case, I'm sure I can find something interesting to do with a whole compound full of big, strong, men," Uma said with a wink.

Battle Lines

Sean watched from the small tower they'd built by the bridge. The defenses had come a long way in the last week; the honey badgers and the wolverines that made up most of the Seabees and the combat engineers they'd gotten had worked like the possessed.

Apparently they'd also infected a fair number of the city's workers and bent their backs to the task. Sean didn't know if those conversions were willing or not, but right now, he really didn't give a damn. There were at least a half million demons coming over the rise in the distance, and they were all headed for the same place.

Reno.

Chad and Maitland had agreed that the best place to put their defensive line was up on McCarran Blvd., Highway 659. It was wide, and it encircled all of Reno. A second defense was being built up on Interstate 80, should the northern end of their defenses on McCarran fail to hold. After that, they'd fall back to the river.

Honestly, if it wasn't for the overwhelming amount of soldiers the djevels had, they probably could hold Reno. There were now over half a million lycans standing in its defense, four thousand of those being lions and lionesses.

They'd overrun his ranch just a few hours ago. Surprisingly they hadn't set it on fire, from what he could tell. Either they didn't know it was his, or they'd just been moving too quickly to realize. He would have bet they'd have torn it all down and destroyed it just because it was his.

The mortar crews all opened up on Chad's command; the enemy was spread too far out to be protected by a shield, but there were still too many of them to cut them all down with artillery. Most of the bombing runs were being done at higher altitudes to give the airplanes a better chance at survival. While they had learned how to armor them against most magical attacks, the closer you were, the more powerful the attack could be, and some things were just too hard to protect against.

But they were working on it.

Every battle was an experience, a learning experience. They were learning the djevels' weak spots, their vulnerabilities, and passing those on to the people whose whole lives were built around designing better weapons and figuring out the tactics of how to use them.

The problem was, the demon lords and princes—or perhaps it was their king—was doing the same thing to them, and while perhaps they weren't being as successful, their troops still came back.

"You know, they're not going to be happy with us after today," Chad said with a smile.

"Chad, right now there are four thousand lions and lionesses who are already unhappy with you. Do you really want to add to that number?" Estrella said from where she was standing next to Sean.

"Oh, they'll get over it."

Sean watched as the leading edge of the djevels came in contract with the barrier on McCarran and spread out along it, taking fire from the soldiers and gun emplacements all along the way. They were dropping pretty heavily.

"We better watch out that they don't stack bodies to climb over the walls," Sean warned.

"If they do that, we'll just set them on fire."

"Then how do we defend them?"

"They're a lot more flammable than we are. We just pull back and wait for that spot to die down," Chad said. He keyed his radio then. "Release the lions!"

Sean sighed. "You've been hanging out with Alex, haven't you?"

"Oh, just a bit. You're just mad because you didn't think of it first!"

Sean watched as two very large groups suddenly came out of cover. One was to the east, the other was to the west, and each had a thousand soldiers in it. Lion soldiers.

The problem they had been facing, however, was how to get the demons to engage the lions. They knew if they were attacked by a lion, the rank and file would have no chance. They also knew they wouldn't come back. Most attacks by the lion infantry groups hadn't been very successful, because the djevels would just flee.

True, the ridders and the biskops would fight, and die, but that was only a small percent of them.

That was when Chad had had one of his more brilliant ideas: the lions would fight in their human forms.

True, none of the lions were happy with the idea. They'd be geared up as regular human soldiers, with human weapons and human armor. They'd keep their faerie swords well-hidden until they ran out of iron bullets, or the enemy was too close to shoot anymore.

But everyone had to admit, the demons probably wouldn't figure it out for days, and anything that had the chance of permanently reducing their numbers was worth doing.

"They're falling for it!" Chad said, and sure enough, the demon army parted like the red sea as it turned to attack the 'foolish humans' taking them on to either side.

Sean watched for a minute. The lion soldiers were concentrating their fire and cutting down the advancing djevels like grass. Their leaders, who had better armor to withstand the iron bullets, were advancing towards the front, swords drawn. They'd be engaging shortly.

"Time for us to attack," Sean said, and with Estrella and Cali following him, he climbed down the tower and joined up with the third group of lions who would be fighting today. Only everyone in this group looked like what they were, lions and lycans. Chad figured if a large group of lions were seen during the fighting today, they wouldn't add two plus two and come to the correct answer.

The gates on the barricade rolled open then, and they sallied forth with Sean in the lead of one group, Maitland in the lead of the other. Sean turned to the west to fall on those engaged with the lions on that side from behind, while Maitland did the opposite. A third group led by Adam moved forward to attack those still coming over the hills.

What Chad and Maitland were looking for was a slaughter. The djevels had become very carefree with their tactics and were spending their minions liberally in each of the fights. Because, after all, they came back.

But with so many lions now in the mix, many would not be coming back, and it would be at least a week before they figured that out. So if they could take a large bite out of the djevel army *now*, it would hopefully pay dividends in the long fight ahead.

They hit the djevels from behind, most of them not even realizing Sean's forces had closed until he was actually attacking them because the noise of the battlefield was so loud. As they attacked, Sean briefly wondered if he could prevail on the horse clan to allow themselves to be used as mounts? They would definitely give Sean's troops a speed and height advantage in combat, and of course they could always join in the fight once their maneuverability was no longer needed.

Of course, Clyde probably wouldn't care much for that idea...

The fighting started off as the very slaughter Chad was wanting. Chad had lined up a solid six thousand troops to ride through the gates, and now that the front lines were engaged, he'd be calling in the battalions Jack was leading off to the east. Rather than bring them into Reno to help in its defense, Chad had left them free to roam the countryside, for now. Mostly he was using them to divert any groups that might decide to head eastward. Eventually they would have to come into the city's defenses, or risk being defeated in detail by the much larger djevel army.

But first, that army would have to figure out where they were.

It didn't take them long to destroy the group that had gone after the lions to the west. Once done, using his radio, Sean called Sampson, who was leading the group, and ordered him to turn to the north to join forces with Adam's group, which was attacking the army that was still continuing to come over the hills.

"Chad! How's Jack doing?" Sean radioed.

"He's destroying their left flank," Chad radioed back. "He's cutting down through Spanish Springs.

See if you can't start a flanking action on their right flank over there. If we can cut them off from the rest of their army, Maitland and Jack can crush them in Sun Valley."

"Won't we be exposed to a flanking attack of our own?" Sean asked as his now combined forces attacked the group Adam was fighting, taking the pressure off his left.

"Once you, Sampson, and Adam get them running, Maitland's group will slide in with the lions on the east, and you'll both turn to the northwest to deal with the forces coming down 395."

"Just us?"

"Don't go past Panther Valley, I got ordnance on the way!"

"Everyone, keep an eye on our left flank!" Sean ordered as he stepped forward to join the fight, Estrella and Cali watching his flanks as he engaged the råge in front of him. There was a biskop approaching quickly, but he seemed uncertain of where to attack, considering the number of lions now on the front line.

Sean pushed forward in an attempt to get to him, but a lioness he didn't recognize got there first and made quick work of him with her sword, impressing Sean with her technique. He often forgot that some of them had been using swords for longer than western civilization had existed.

Continuing to fight, he felt it before he heard it, the ground shaking under his feet. Apparently Chad's ordnance had arrived. He had no idea how long it had taken to get there, he was just happy that it had. The group they were fighting were now trying to retreat back along 395 as Maitland's forces drove though like a wedge and forced the larger part of the army towards Jack's troops.

"We got trouble on the left flank, Sean!" Sampson called over the radio.

"Adam, we're pivoting!" Sean called and then gave the order for everyone to reform, pulling back from the enemy and allowing them to flee as they reorganized. Adam's troops moved up Sean's reforming right flank, pushing the quickly dwindling force there back and engaging them in Sean's place as Sean trotted up to the new front of his formation, panting heavily.

"What's wrong?" he called as he made his way forward. The men on his left flank were now fighting a new foe, and he noticed suddenly that the bombs dropping from up above were deflecting to either side of the highway and hitting the hills. They were still doing a lot of damage to the army coming down the road, but more than half were still coming.

"I think we have a demon lord!" Sampson called.

Sean swore loudly.

"I'm coming!" he called and moved quickly towards Sampson. When he got there, he noticed that Howart was there, along with a few other lions Sean didn't know the names of, but whom he recognized.

"Great!" Sampson said. "If you can keep his magic off of us, we'll take him down."

"Huh?" Sean said, blinking. "That's a demon lord!"

"Yup, and I've got five dollars on being the one to kill him!" Sampson growled. "Flying wedge! Let's do this!"

Sean noticed then that the *entire* front line was lions, even if they were in human form, and they took off at a slow jog, cutting through the advancing enemy with a will. Sean immediately cast a large shield spell before them as they moved, to deflect any magical attacks.

"Adam! Better move up behind us!" Sean ordered.

"On it!" Adam radioed back.

Looking up, the demon lord saw Sean at the same time Sean saw him, and Sean unleashed a flurry of magic missiles and fireballs at same time the lord cast a bunch of spells at him.

Sean was then busy deflecting, or absorbing, those spells as they continued to move forward quickly.

Seeing a single lion in the group approaching him, the lord apparently felt secure enough that he started to move forward as well.

"You will not find me so easy to kill as you did Holigart, Lion! I shall be eating *you* this night!"

"And to which prince shall I send my regrets when you are dead, fool?" Sean yelled back and threw a flame strike to clear the area around the lord of any defenders.

"He's one of Skarm's," Estrella said in a loud whisper.

"Come! Come to me and die! Foolish Lion!"

At that point, Sampson stepped up and engaged him, with Howart on his right and the other lion on his left. The rest of the line kept pushing, using the clearing Sean's last spell had given them.

"Die, foolish mortals!" The lord screamed and attacked.

"Who are you calling 'mortal', scumbag!" Sampson yelled back, and suddenly the demon lord found three lions attacking him.

"Sucker!" Estrella yelled, and Sean had the pleasure of witnessing absolute fear on the demon lord's face as all three lions attacked him simultaneously. The lord fought furiously, but he was seriously outmatched, and started taking damage immediately. Sean watched him heal himself once before Howart took off his left arm as he blocked Sampson's thrust to his face.

The lord then made the mistake of turning to face Sampson and Howart, leaving the third lion to slip behind him and hamstring him. As he went down, both Sampson and Howart lunged forward with their swords, one taking him high, the other low, and he fell to the ground, dead.

With the lord's death, the shield spell that had been protecting the marching army came down, and bombs fell amongst them once again. This time Sean was forced to throw a shield above his own troops, doing what he could to deflect the bombs towards the attacking djevels.

"Back! Everyone back!" Estrella called as Sean concentrated on the spell, doing his best not to stumble as they retreated.

"What's going on over there?" Chad called.

"Demon lord, he's dead now," Cali radioed back while Sean continued to burn energy on the shield until finally they were far enough away that he could drop it.

"Damn, that was hard!" he said, panting. "How the hell do they keep it up so long?"

"Don't ask me, I'm not a magic user," Estrella told him.

"What's our next fight, Chad?"

"Right now you don't have one. Pull back to base and we'll see what develops. Maitland and Jack are obliterating the part of the army they cut off. Once they're done, we'll see what how it goes."

"Sounds good. Okay everyone, back to the staging area."

"So how'd your people do?" Chad asked as Sean caught up with him at his command post.

"We only took about ten percent on the casualties," Sean said with a sigh as he dropped his tired butt into one of the folding camp chairs set by the table where Chad was going over troop movements.

"I meant the lions, how many did you lose?"

"Oh, not many, seven of them. They'll be back in about a week."

Sean chuckled as Chad gave a quiet fist pump.

"That's some of the best news I've heard all day. Now if only we had more of them!"

"Well, right now I think they need them more in South American than we do here."

"They're not going to take any of the ones here away, are they?"

Sean shook his head. "No. Those are ours; they're staying here. Honestly, a *lot* of the lions wanted to stay here. A lot of them have never seen a modern city, and they like the conveniences."

"How does that happen?" Chad asked, looking up from his maps.

Sean shrugged. "A lot of the lions haven't been here in a couple hundred years, or longer. They've been keeping the numbers down. Not sure that's going to continue, though."

"The old 'now that they've seen the big city, how are you going to keep them down on the farm', story?"

"More like there's a lot more lycans in the world now, and someone has to keep an eye on them so they don't get out of hand," Sean said with a smirk. "Lion la-la land is a pretty nice place."

"Lion la-la land? Another technical term?" Chad asked with a chuckle.

"Eh, seems as good a name as any, seeing as no one ever thought to give it a name."

"It's not the 'lion home world' then?"

"Earth is the lion home world. We own it, lock stock and barrel. We just let the humans run it because they've done so much with the place!" Sean said, waving his hands around with a grin.

"After two world wars and all the other messes we've made, I'm surprised they'd believe that."

"Trust me, I know the stories. We were worse, a *lot* worse."

Chad paused a moment, then looked over at Sean. "You're a lion now; it's finally become who you are, hasn't it?"

Sean nodded slowly. "Yeah, it has. I've stopped thinking about it as me and them; it's all just 'us' now. It hasn't *fully* settled in; there are still a few things I'm having trouble grappling with. Some ideas that my mind keeps shying away from."

"Oh? Such as?"

"Immortality. I mean, apparently we all have it to some degree or other; humans and lycans have souls that go, well, *somewhere* after you die. But lions? We're here for pretty much ever."

"You sure on the soul thing?"

"That's what the djevels eat, so yeah, I'm sure on the soul thing. I've even seen a couple. I suspect the First knows more about it than I do, but I'm hesitant to ask. So!" Sean sat up and clapped his hands, changing the subject. "How'd we do today?"

"We did well. I'm estimating we killed over two hundred thousand of the enemy."

"That many?"

"They've been pretty careless. Because they keep coming back, they have no fear, so slaughtering them by job lots isn't all that hard."

"When about half those killed today don't come back, that's going to change, you know."

Chad smiled. "I'm counting on it."

"Really?"

"Of course! Soldiers who have no fear of death are the most dangerous. They don't hesitate, and they don't stop until you've killed them. Soldiers who are afraid of their own mortality? They hesitate, they don't take chances, they have to be spurred on. Especially when they're something as self-centered and uncaring as the demons we've been fighting. So if we can put the fear of death into them, it slows them down and makes our fight easier."

"I really need to go back and talk to Mahkiyoc about those weapons, don't I?"

Chad nodded in agreement, a grim expression on his face. "Yeah, you do."

"Well, we've got the weapons, and we're working on armor for our teams. I'll get everyone together tonight and see what's left to do. Then we'll just have to wait on the next gateway."

"And hope it's somewhere they don't have control over."

"We still have that bomb I had you plant at the main gateway. If we need to, we can set that off first as a diversion and make it look like we're trying to take it back."

Chad looked thoughtful a moment. "That'd work. I better put together an attack plan to go with it so they think we're serious."

Standing up, Sean took a look at the maps on the table, and the markers Chad had place on it.

"How long until they try to take Reno again?"

"I think we have a week. More, if they decide they want to build up a larger force. It won't be until they realize we're whittling them down faster than they're whittling us down that they'll move to an overwhelming force."

Sean nodded and headed towards the exit.

"Oh! Before I forget, the tac-nukes showed up a few hours ago."

"Well, that sounds auspicious," Sean said with a frown. "Gonna mine Reno?"

"Adam had a long conversation with me about 'food supplies'," Chad said, making finger quotes. "He thought it would be better if he gave me the talk than it would be if you did."

"I thought we already had that conversation?" Sean said, blinking in surprise.

"We did, but Adam drove it home with a couple of very dire threats. Even offered to give the order for me, if necessary, so I wouldn't have it on my conscience."

"He didn't?" Sean growled. He didn't like it when people threatened his friends.

"He did, and I took him up on it. So don't go getting your panties in a bunch. We talked about it, but he drove it home, and I'm honestly thankful he's willing to take the heat on it. Sending soldiers out to die is one thing, but killing civilians? Even if it's to protect them from something worse than death?"

Chad shook his head. "No, I can't do that, and I'm happy he offered."

"I could do it for you," Sean offered.

Chad laughed. "I wouldn't let you do it, Sean, even if I thought you could. Like you said, there are still things you're coming to grips with. Well, Adam isn't."

Sean dropped his head and sighed. Chad was right.

"Later."

"Later."

Heading out of the command post, Sean rounded up the girls as they found a ride back to their base. He really needed a shower.

"Dae, I need a favor."

"Sure, what is it?"

"I want a bunch of my bombs made, but these need to be smaller and more portable. Put the tags and bars in them. They also can't have any electronics in them."

Daelyn nodded. "I can do that, is windup okay?"

"That'd be fine."

"Give me a couple of days. I'll have to stop by my uncle's for the parts, but I can build it. Will six be enough?"

"Make it eight."

"Got it!"

Into the Breech

"So now what?" Roxy asked Sean as he dropped onto the couch, still damp from showering.

"Now I need to go have an argument with Dad." Sean sighed, closing his eyes and leaning back into the cushions.

"You mean the First?"

Sean nodded.

"Over what?"

"Going through a gateway."

"Doesn't he want to go?"

"He doesn't want to go *now*. I think he's still mad at me for figuring out how to pull his ass out of lion la-la land."

"Maybe he just doesn't like it that you figured out something he hadn't?"

Sean snorted. "He's a crafty old bastard. I'm not so sure he didn't know about it. The problem is, sometimes his ideas about what's right and what's best are just *wrong*."

"Ah! The voice of teenaged wisdom!" Roxy teased.

"I'm not a teenager anymore, Rox," Sean said with a growl. "Yeah, I'm still young, I get that. But he's just as bad at the other end of the spectrum. Thousands of years of wisdom and experience! But unfortunately, he's like your grandfather trying to figure out a cellphone, or how to use the internet. Things have changed, a *lot*. The time for new things is here, *now*. I'm not willing to let half the world get destroyed, or even a little bit of it.

"We don't live in the fuckin' stone age anymore! It took hundreds of years to get where we are today, maybe a thousand! I don't even want to drop back into the nineteen fifties of technology, much less the eighteen fifties! We've got to act now if we don't want to end up living in some sort of shitty post-apocalyptic world!"

"Would that really be such a bad thing?" The First's voice came from over by the door.

Rolling over onto his knees and facing him over the back of the couch, Sean growled back at him.

"Yes! It would be! How many people do you think would die from a lack of clean water? Hell, would we even be able to grow enough food? And when winter comes, no electricity, no light, no *heat*! Dammit, Dad! You keep saying humans did such a great job with the place that we have to help them along! So why the *fuck* aren't you helping?"

The First blinked. "Not helping?" he said with a growl of his own. "What do you think I've been doing? Where do you think you came from? Why do you think I had you infected? Why do you think I was in your head? Why did I have Sampson track down your father?

"I've been helping for tens of thousands of years! Don't come off telling me that I haven't been helping, *Son*!"

Roxy noticed that the First had taken several steps into the room and was now almost nose to nose with Sean. She also noticed that Keairra and Dienna were by the door and motioning to her to come to them. Dodging around Sean and the First, she made for the doorway.

"Oh, right, *helping*!" Sean growled back. "Two thirds of the lions are off on holiday enjoying a never-ending party instead of being back here building up defenses and getting ready!"

"There weren't enough lycans to support us all!"

"You could have made enough! It's a big country! Hell, it's a big *planet*!"

"Without a cure for silver, the mages would have killed us all! We would have been powerless against the demons! We didn't know if your father would find the answer, so we had to make choices, *hard* choices!"

"Hard choices? *You* had to make hard choices? My *life* has been nothing but hard choices!" Sean yelled back at him. "You were just sitting on your ass on a mountainside. Well, now it's time for you to get *off* your ass and go to work! Hard choices my *ass*!"

Keairra pulled the door closed and took Roxy by the elbow. "Let's go get some coffee while they work this one out."

"Are you sure it's safe?" Roxy asked, looking back at the closed door.

"Of course it is, just as long as we're far enough away," Keairra said with a laugh. "This has been coming for a while. The First has been taking Sean for granted at times and not listening to him."

"And Sean's been doing the same with the First," Dienna added with a laugh of her own. "They're about due."

"Due for what?" Roxy asked worriedly as they retreated away from the yelling coming through the door.

"A leveling of the playing field."

"So," Sean continued, "just what was this '*hard* choice'? Which stupid lackey to get to do your dirty work?"

The First shook his head and narrowed his eyes, growling slightly. "No, it was how much of North America we were going to nuke."

Sean flinched, pulling back a little. "What?"

"The cold war, the nuclear build up. You don't think that happened all by itself, do you? No, we helped that along. We knew the next gateway was going to drop right in the middle of one of the biggest population centers in the world. South America we could handle. But North America? No, we couldn't.

"So, we made a plan. *I* made a plan," the First growled, taking another step forward. "I decided if we couldn't figure out the silver problem, if our children were still under the thrall of the mages, we'd carpet nuke the US and kill everyone. Kill as many demons as possible and deny them the entire food supply! If we had too many lions out when *that* happened, we'd have another die off, and then *no one* would be left to defend the rest of the world!

"So yes, *Son*, I've been making some very *hard* choices, and it hasn't been easy!"

"Why didn't you tell me about it? Why didn't you tell me about the gateway!"

"I didn't know about the gateway..."

Sean hauled off and punched the First right in the side of his muzzle, turning his head to the side.

The First blinked and looked at him. "What the hell was that for?"

"For not telling me the truth! For holding out on me!" Sean yelled, thinking about the episode with the US Marshals.

"Son, there are things you're just not meant to know. There are things no one is meant to know beyond the First Pride," the First said in a calm voice.

"Bullshit, Dad!" Sean yelled back. "You know what I carry around up here," Sean said, pointing to his own head, "you were *there* when I learned it! All of it! Spells that can cause so much destruction and so much harm that I tore pages out of my father's spell book and *burned* them."

"Sean..."

"No! No more bullshit, no more holding out. You need to tell me everything!" Sean said, raising a fist, ready to punch him again.

"You're too young."

Sean punched him, or tried to at least. The First dodged and punched him in the side, and with that, the fight was on. Sean knew he wasn't as experienced as the First was, but he didn't care; he was hella pissed, and he was going to lay the biggest smackdown on him that he'd ever gotten.

When it was finally over, they were both lying on the ground, panting. All of the furniture in the room had been reduced to scrap, and there were several holes in the walls now. Sean's entire body hurt. He had no idea how the First was feeling, other than tired, but at least he'd knocked him down, twice!

Of course the First had knocked Sean down about a dozen times, but that hadn't stopped him, not once.

"Feel better now, Son?"

Sean sighed. "Tell me, Dad. Tell me everything."

"Let's not start this again," the First said with a wince.

"Tell. Me. Everything. I've earned it, and you can *not* deny it."

"Give me one good reason."

"Other than getting your ass kicked again?" Sean growled.

The First laughed. "I don't think this counts as getting my ass kicked. Sorry, Son."

Sean rolled over and faced the First, looking into his eyes. "Then how about because I understand a lot of this more than you do? Deep down, you're still just a lion, Dad. Yeah, you've had hundreds of thousands of years to come to terms with your intelligence, with being self-aware, all that shit.

"But I started out as a man. I was trained in a world of science and facts, not mysteries and superstitions."

"Oh? And what about magic?"

"If there wasn't a science to it, Dad, I wouldn't be able to cheat at it as much as I do. It still follows the rules; it just has a few extra ones that no one knows about."

The First nodded slowly. "Okay, I'll buy that. We're part demon, Son."

"*What*!"

"We're part demon. That's why they can't affect us, and why they can't affect anything bred from us. At least not the way they can with humans. We're part and parcel a piece of them, so they can't use those powers on us. It's the very same reason we can kill them."

"How? How can that be?"

"When we found Mahkiyoc Aan Drues' friend, he wasn't alone. He was fighting with a demon prince. Fighting badly, I might add. But best I can figure it out, he had one of those weapons with him, so he had done a fair bit of damage to the prince before it had stopped working."

"And?"

The First laughed. "And we killed and ate them both!"

Sean sighed.

"Oh, come on, we were lions and they were both made out of meat, what did you expect us to do?"

"I've tasted demon, Dad. How in the hell did you stomach *that*?"

The First shrugged. "We'd eaten worse. Plus I think eating that alien helped. Eventually the demon started to turn into one of those puddles, but we'd already eaten the best parts, so we just finished up with the other one."

Sean remembered something. "I thought you didn't remember what happened?"

"Yeah, I lied. One of the few things any of us in the First Pride lie about. We didn't want anyone to know what happened." The First looked over at Sean. "And honestly? Until you talked to Mahkiyoc, we had no idea who or what he was, though we did eventually figure out the demon prince.

"Again, we didn't know the why of it, and for a long, long time it didn't even occur to us to wonder about it. When we finally started to fight the demons, well, we figured out half of it. But not the other half."

Sean digested that a minute. "And until Estrella and I came back, you had no idea you could survive on any plane other than Earth."

"Pretty much."

"And what about the lion la-la land?"

The First shrugged again. "I don't know. For millennia I thought it was something that existed purely in our heads. We can manipulate most things there by thought. It wasn't until you opened that gateway and Sampson went through that we even knew travel from it was possible."

"What about those two US Marshals?"

"I pulled you in to the fringes of it and then sent you back. You were already alive. So were they. The only thing Keairra, I, and the rest can figure out is, like the demons, when we're killed, we respawn. We just do it in our own private reality. Now that we can gate through to the Earth, well, death is only temporary. Assuming we *can* be killed."

Sean blinked at that. "What?"

"Son, we're gods. And with the number of lycans alive in the world today, you're going to find out that you don't age, you don't get sick, and you don't die. True, with modern weapons it probably will be possible to kill one of us now, unlike when I was younger. But again, so what? We respawn, then we gate back in."

"I...I had no idea..."

"Welcome to immortality," the First said with a sigh. "Trust me, it's not always as great as people think it is. That's why I didn't want to come back, why I wanted to stay there."

"Huh?"

"Son, I have lost so many lovers and friends to the sands of time that I don't want to lose anymore. It's easier for some, but I'm the First, the alpha male, the head of the pride. It's my job to keep everyone safe and alive. Losing people to the ravages of time, even if they're not lions, it still hurts."

"I had no idea, Dad."

"Well, we better get up and go find the others. I'm sure they think we've killed each other by now."

Sean nodded and got back to his feet, slowly. The First had definitely given him a lot to think about.

"Would you really have destroyed the world?"

"The world, no. A part of it?" The First took Sean's hand as Sean pulled him to his feet. "You have to understand, Son, just how old I am and how much I've seen. Sure, it'd set the world back hundreds of years. So what? That's like a good night's sleep to me now."

"You've gotten hidebound, Dad." Sean said. "We need to do this. *We* may be immortal, but all the others? They're not. Civilization is most definitely not. We got a good thing going right now, if we don't protect it, save it, who's to say what comes next is going to be anything worth dying for?"

The First sighed. "Maybe you're right."

"Course I'm right!" Sean said with a weak laugh. "But honestly, we just might have a chance to end this, end it once and for all. Wouldn't it be better to take that chance now, before things have gone too far, than to wait until we're desperate and grasping at straws?"

"Let's go get some food, and I'll gather the others together and we'll talk about it."

"See?" Keairra said to Roxy as Sean and the First walked into the mess. "They survived."

"This happen often?"

"Let's just say they have a bit of a contentious relationship at times. The First isn't used to anyone standing up to him anymore and, well," Keairra and Dienna both grinned, "Sean doesn't take shit from anybody anymore, not even him."

"I think he likes it," Dienna added.

Keairra laughed. "Yeah, but he won't admit it, not to anyone. Sean's the son he always wanted."

"Living together in the same head probably had something to do with that," Roxy speculated.

"Most likely," Dienna agreed. "Sean's got no fear of him, that's for sure, and he's made some pretty dire threats to Sean."

"Really?" Roxy blinked.

"And Sean just gets right back in his face for it!" Keairra laughed. "We've all made it clear, me and the other wives that is, that if he so much as hurts a hair on his son's head, we are going to spend the next ten thousand years making his life complete misery."

"Well, thanks for that, I guess." Roxy said.

Dienna shrugged. "When it comes to Sean, he's more bluster than threat. I don't know that we really needed to spell it out for him."

"I do," Keairra said with a smug grin. "He can be dense at times."

Sean and the First dropped down into seats at the table.

"What are you all talking about?" the First asked.

"You, Dear," Keairra said with a grin.

"Good, as it should be. Now would you be a good little wife and get your starving mate some food?"

"What, your legs don't work?" Keairra teased.

"Puleeeeaaasssssseeee?" the First said with such a soulful and pathetic look on his face that Roxy couldn't help herself and started laughing, loudly.

Keairra sighed loudly and got up. "You'd starve to death without us, you know."

When the First made his lower lip tremble, Roxy fell out of her chair.

"Such a conman!" Dienna snickered and got up as well.

"Where in the hell did you learn how to do that?" Sean asked, eyes wide in shock.

"Disney movies. I may be old, but I'm not stupid." The First snickered, softly, then looked at Roxy on the floor. "You going to be alright down there?"

"Give me a minute," Roxy said, still gasping. "That wasn't fair."

"Course it wasn't. Now go get your mate some food, or I'll break out the big guns."

Roxy scrambled to her feet quickly. "I don't think I'd survive!" she said, still snickering as she went off to get Sean some food.

"So, now that you two got all that out of your system," Keairra said after she, Dienna, and Roxy had delivered their food, "what have you decided?"

"We're going to talk about going through the gateway. Sean wants to go now, and I'm willing to consider it."

Keairra nodded. "Who's going?"

"I was thinking all of the Pride."

"All of them? Raban's in Germany, Denup and Ing are in South America, and your sister is still in China."

"And Reagjin is keeping an eye on Africa, I know. Everyone else. They're all here, or will be soon at any rate."

"I was thinking three teams," Sean began.

The First shook his head. "Two. You, me, the rest of the Pride, whoever you want, and maybe a few others will be in the first team. We'll be the ones looking for these 'weapons' of yours and having a little talk with Mahkiyoc Aan Drues about his life choices and those of his race."

"Are you sure that's wise?"

"Course I do, I'm your father," the First said and winked.

"The second team will be much larger, mostly F2s, maybe some other lycans to balance them out. They'll be the ones running around and attacking the demons and making them worry about what's going on in *their* territory. I need to talk with Chad about some sort of diversions while we're in there. He's got a quick mind, I'm sure he'll have some good advice."

Sean gasped theatrically, putting a hand to his chest. "You do take advice! Oh my god! It's the end of the world!!"

The First sighed and shook his head. "Keep working on it, your sarcasm still needs practice."

"So when are we going?" Roxy asked.

The First shrugged, then scowled at Roxy. "Did you just kick me?"

"Yup, now when are we going?"

"Young lady, I'll..." The First turned and looked at Keairra, who was suddenly looking innocently at the ceiling.

"Okay, fine. We will discuss this after we've gotten the Pride together and everyone has had a chance to speak."

"So, soon then?"

The First rolled his eyes and looked at Sean. "Well, at least now I know where you get it from."

"Oh, please, I got it from you when you lived in my head," Sean said with a grin.

"He's got you there, Dear," Keairra said.

"Uh-huh. Just let me eat in peace and then we can gather everyone up."

Sean looked around the room; the First was there with his wives, Keairra, Saf'kij, Jipouet, Peym, Nibisa, and Sasha, as well as a bunch of others he didn't know. Doing a quick headcount, Sean got eighteen who were going in this team.

Sean started off introducing his wives, "This is Roxy, Daelyn, Jolene, Roberta, Peg, Cali, and Estrella. Daelyn, Roberta, and Jolene will be staying here, so they won't be on either team. And the rest of you are?"

"These are Wendy, Mincibi, Rowan, Libmanov, and Kalif," Keairra said, pointing each of them out.

Sean and his wives nodded and said hello. Kalif was the only lion; the other four were all lionesses.

"So they're...?" Roxy asked, looking over at the First's wives.

"Our Cubs," Sasha said with a huge grin.

Peg snickered. "Must suck to have to be called 'cubs' for all eternity!"

"Eh, it's not like we don't do the same to our own kids," Libmanov said. "And call me Libby."

"Okay," Sean said, tapping the chart on the wall. "As you can see, we're coming up to the twenty-fourth, which means a new window. If we don't take that gateway, we won't have another one until after the thirtieth, as we're about to hit the second non-gate interval."

"Well, let's go grab our gear and get ready to go," Rowan said.

"Hold on," the First said, raising his hand. "We haven't decided if we're going to go or not. We're going to talk it out first."

"Oh, come *on* father! We've been talking about this for the last hundred thousand years. We all want to go, even you. So let's just gear up and get ready. Esti did it, so we can do it too."

"Really, Dad," Kalif spoke up next. "How long can it take? We go, see if we can find this Mahkiyoc guy, and find out what he's got for us, and what he can do. Esti's been there, it'll take what? A few days?"

"And then what?" the First asked, looking at his children.

"Who knows? It's not like we can make plans until *after* we find out what he can do for us. Worse comes to worst, I say we just eat him like his friend and move on."

"Eat him?" Jolene said with a bit of a sour expression.

"Hey, he and his unleashed this mess on us," Wendy growled. "I don't see any reason to leave the bastard alive when all is said and done. Do you?"

"Umm..." Jolene blushed. "You may have a point there."

"Course she does!" Daelyn said with a laugh.

The First sighed and looked at his wives, who were all sitting there quietly smiling.

"And?" he asked looking at them.

"We've already picked a team of forty for the other group. We sent them off to get armor and weapons," Peym said.

"They do this to you often?" Sean asked in a loud whisper.

"More than I like to admit," the First admitted with a sigh. "Yours?"

"All the time," Sean said with a grin.

"Does anyone know what's happening on the other side of one of these small gates now?" Wendy asked, looking around.

Roxy nodded. "We've been sending teams through to do a quick look and then jump back out. Usually there's a group of about a hundred bonde, with a pair of råge to keep them under control, and then a ridder and a biskop in charge of the whole thing."

"That's it?"

"You have to understand, Sis," Estrella said, "they have no idea where a gate is going to open. There's about fifty different helliges, which is what they call the gate anchors, that a gateway can open up at. That's a lot of ground to cover, and King Sladd isn't known for being the most imaginative leader. Besides, it's not like anyone has *ever* tried to invade before."

"The djevels invaded, didn't they?"

Estrella snorted. "Until Mahkiyoc told me that, I thought they'd always been there, because they believe they've always been there. They're clever, and they're cunning, but they're not the smartest. They never figured out I was a lion, even though I killed them, ate them, and couldn't be affected by them, because I was female and didn't have a mane."

"Point," Wendy said with a duck of her head.

"Has anyone explained the weapons to you?" Sean asked.

Saf'kij raised a hand. "I've used ones like this before. So have Jipouet and Sasha. We'll make sure the others are trained tonight."

"Oh?"

"Unlike our mate over there, some of us *like* coming back and checking out the world," Saf'kij said, grinning.

"Most of us, actually," Keairra added. "But most of the weapons the humans have come up with in the last several hundred years, we haven't all had the chance to play with them."

Sean nodded. "So, I'll tell Chad to task us six Black Hawks so we can get out there as soon as the next gate opens?"

"I haven't said we're doing this yet!" the First growled.

Everyone turned and looked at him, and Sean got the distinct impression if he said no this time, that would be it.

"Well, Dear?" Keairra asked. "Are we going? Because you know we all want to. We've all been wanting to do this for far too long."

The First sighed. "Nice to see *somebody* still values my opinion!"

There were a number of raspberries from the other six wives at that comment, Sean noticed.

"But yes, you're right. I've been dying for the opportunity to see if we can't finally do something about these rude little monsters who think they have a right to mess with that which is *ours*. We're going."

Highway to Hell

Sean looked out the windscreen of the helicopter. They were cruising a hundred feet over the desert, going about as fast as a Black Hawk could go. It wasn't the kind of trip that made for a comfortable flight, either, as they often banked up to go around, rather than over, any obstacle that showed up before them.

Trey was fully concentrating on not running into anything; it was past two in the morning, and they were running without lights. Sean also had silence spells cast on all the helicopters before they left. The gateway they wanted was only five miles from the main gateway. The last thing they wanted was to draw any defenders from the fort there.

The gateway had opened less than twenty minutes ago, on the last day of the current window. They'd been ready for days now, and the waiting had been getting to all of them. There are only so many times you can check your equipment, inspect your weapons, and go over your plans. When the report of the gate opening came, they'd all cheered.

His headset came to life.

"Lion One, Lion One, this is Angel Three. We're seeing activity at the fort."

"What kind of activity?" Sean asked. Angel Three was a very high-flying jet with a crew of several reconnaissance experts. They had cameras, radar, and all sorts of tricks up there.

"They're scrambling, running around. Something's got them excited. Looks like they're manning the defenses."

"Guess they know you're coming," Chad broadcast from his position back at the base. "Angel

Three, Home Base. Does it look like they're putting together an attack force?"

"Home Base, it looks like they're forming up troops to the northwest of the fort. But that's all we can tell from up here."

Sean looked at the panel of their GPS unit. They were still twenty minutes out from their target. They could disembark, form up, and go through the gateway in five minutes, ten max. But the helicopters wouldn't be able to stay and pull them out if stuff on the other side of the gateway went bad if there was a group on the way from the main gateway. They could make it close enough in a half hour to force the helicopters not to stick around, or they'd be lost.

"Pass the order, Chad. Pull everyone back! Tell 'em to run or dig a deep hole!"

Sean switched to the intercom. "Trey! Pass the word, we need to stop and land!"

Sean heard Trey pass the word to the helicopters strung out behind him to be prepared to stop and land.

"What's up, Boss?" Trey asked, as they slowed.

"We need cover. A big hill or something between us and them." Sean pointed to a likely spot on the GPS. "There's good."

"Cover from what?"

"Air blast," Sean told him.

Sean blinked as Trey said something over the radio, spun the helicopter sideways, tilted it up, and then dropped them down behind a hill, putting the wheels on the ground, the main rotor still spinning. Looking out past Trey, he could see the other five Black Hawks doing the same thing.

"Lion One! They're starting to move out."

"Chad! Sixty second warning! Tell everyone to dig in, now!" Sean called.

Leaning back in his seat, Sean closed his eyes and checked his levels, then started putting the trigger spell together as he counted down loudly.

When he hit zero, he fired off the spell, watching with his mind's eye as it made a beeline over the hills and the valleys until it hit the small exposed wire that led down to the box he'd had Chad bury over a month ago.

"Heads down! Close your eyes!" Sean warned over the radio, and a moment after that, it was daylight outside. Three hundred and fifty ounces of silver suddenly were subjected to magically-induced alpha decay as the physical laws regarding the strong nuclear force were suddenly tweaked in all those bars, simultaneously, for less than a pico-second, and all that energy was released instantaneously in one *very* large explosion.

Just then the helicopter's engine seemed to rev up, and he could almost feel it pressing down harder into the ground beneath as the light faded. He could hear Trey counting out loud, "…five, one mile, seven, eight, nine, ten, eleven, two mile, thirteen…"

When he hit two hundred and forty seconds, they all heard it, possibly the loudest explosion of Sean's life, the helicopter slid backward across the ground as Trey fought the controls, and then suddenly they were climbing up out from behind the hill, fast.

"Everyone okay?" Sean called over the radio.

"Lion Two, Okay!"

"Lion Three, Okay!"

"Lion Four, I think we're gonna need some downtime, but we're good!"

"Lion Five, I'm down! Sheered the tail rotor!"

"Lion Six, coming back around to Lion Five!"

"Lion Five, offload, we'll divide everyone between the remaining aircraft!" Sean ordered as Trey banked, then up and around.

"Gonna be crowded back here," Roxy said with a sigh.

"Better than the alternative," Estrella said.

"Angel Three," Sean called over the radio. "Do you think that got their attention?"

"Lion One, hold on, we're still changing out our sensors, but best I can tell, there ain't nothing left down there but a big ass hole."

"Well, that'll definitely keep them busy then." Sean sighed and watched as Trey brought them in behind Lion Four, which was now taking on some of Lion Five's troops and gear. Lion Six was hovering just to the east.

Ten minutes later they were back on course, a little slower due to the extra weight.

"Situation report, Angel Three?" Sean called.

"Looks like every djevel in the area is heading for the main gateway as fast as they can."

"Chad?" Sean called.

"I can confirm that, from what our outposts and ground troops are seeing. They're moving back to defend the gateway. I've already ordered up a fire mission; shells will be landing all around there any moment now. We're executing a counterattack as well.

"Just how big of an explosion was that, Sean?" Estrella asked.

"A kiloton, give or take a little."

"What's a 'kiloton'?"

"Overkill," Sean said with a smile.

"Overkill is good," Trey said. "Though I suspect someone is gonna be upset with you for Lion Five."

"Well, hopefully they can fix it before the djevels find it, but right now I suspect they have other things to worry about."

"True dat."

Sean continued to check in with Angel Three for the next twenty minutes as they made their way to the gate. Nobody was headed that way, and the small team watching it from a nearby hilltop wasn't reporting any activity, either.

Trey swung around and came in, landing them behind the gate. It took a minute longer to get out because of the extra people and gear, but ten minutes later, they were forming up and circling around to the front of the gate. Sean checked his watch; it had been open for forty-nine minutes.

"Well, no time like the present." Looking around, Sean motioned to the group of F2s who were being led by Trevor, a lion Sean had only recently met. They'd all agreed that the second team would go through first and secure the area, then Sean and the First's team would come through.

The only thing Sean wasn't sure about at this point was who led his team, him or the First. The First was still the ultimate authority, but since they'd been alerted on the gate opening, Sean had been the one giving all the orders.

As they watched, Trevor led his team through at a trot, weapons loaded and ready. As the last one went through, Sean checked his watch. If no one came back out in five minutes, the mission would probably be scrubbed.

Three minutes later, Jesse, the lioness who was second in command, popped back out.

"The råge and the ridder are dead; so are most of the bonde. We're still fighting the biskop."

"Sounds good enough to me," Sean said and looked at the First, who was carrying duel shotguns, both of which were sawed off even shorter than what the dwarves had given them.

"Let's go," the First growled, and with that, Sean charged through the gateway with the rest of the team on his heels.

Sean blinked as he stepped out onto the ramp; this was the same hellige he and Estrella had been at before! Running down the ramp, he broke to the right as they spread out to cover the ground. The Biskop was dead; apparently whoever had been fighting him hadn't had too many difficulties. There weren't any bonde left, either.

Sean did a quick check of the small blockhouse he and Estrella had been living in, with her and Roxy tagging along to make sure it was clear. Then they met up near the hole in the palisades Sean and Estrella had escaped from last time.

Trevor and his team were gathering near the spot where the gate in the palisade used to be. Sean wasn't all that surprised no one had fixed it. As he watched, Trevor sent out his scouts. From this point, both teams were on their own, so there really wasn't any point in talking to them.

"Wow, this is freaky," Peg said, looking around. "It's like one of those old movies my grandparents used to watch."

"I know, right?" Roxy said, looking around. "I think the only stuff that has any color on it is what we brought, and even that's pretty muted."

"It's the light," Sean said, "it's gray during the day, and I think actually black at night."

"How can light be black?" Peg asked, giving him a strange look.

Sean shrugged. "Beats me. This whole place is strange. Did you notice that inside the blockhouse, even though there aren't any lights, it's never dark?"

"Now that you mention it..."

Sean turned to Cali then, who looked...different.

"How are you doing, Hon?"

"I feel a little different," Cali said. "I'm not sure I can quite explain it. Like there is something I am missing that I can now have, if only I knew what it was."

Sean looked her over; her hair had a strange luster to it, and her ears seemed longer, her teeth sharper, and did she have fangs now?

"Something wrong with Cali?" the First asked, coming over.

"She says she feels different, and she even looks a little different."

The First shrugged. "Dark elves are rumored to be part demon, probably why they like killing them so much. This place is full of negative energy, so I'm not surprised she's feeling it."

"I'm part djevel?" Cali said, looking at the First in surprise.

"You know elves," the First said with a dramatic sigh, "they'll sleep with anything."

"Wait, what?" Roxy exclaimed, eyes wide. "They slept with demons?"

The First laughed. "Not all the races that come from the negative planes are evil or ugly. There is a myth that dark elves came about because a group fleeing one of the negative planes ended up with a bunch of elves. Couple thousand years later, we have dark elves." The First shrugged. "The

Fædreland lies a lot closer to the negative planes than our world, or even the world of the elves."

"How come I have never heard of this before?" Cali asked, looking a little distressed.

"Obviously because those who fled hated their past and wanted to break from it? It was many tens of thousands of years ago, Cali. It lies dead in the past, don't let it worry you. We all still love you."

Sean took a step forward and gave her a hug to reinforce the First's words.

"Huh, I wonder if she can get wings and horns?" Peg said with a thoughtful look on her face.

"Peggy!" Cali said with a shocked look on her face.

"Oh come on, Cal! With your looks, you'd rock it. Probably need a pry bar to get Sean here off you!" Peg said with a wink.

Sean took half a step back and looked her up and down.

"See? He's already thinking about it!"

Cali blushed, and Sean pulled her back in against him.

"You know, she might just be right about that!" he whispered in her ear and gave her a kiss.

Estrella came over then.

"Anything I need to know about?"

"Cali's part demon," Peg said.

"Really? Well, she doesn't look anything like the ones we have around here." Estrella raised her voice then. "Everyone ready?" She looked around, and when no one said anything, she turned and headed off. "Follow me."

"How far away are we?" Keairra asked Sean, who was bringing up the rear.

"Two or three days. This is the gate we were waiting at last time. We did it in two, but we ran for most of that 'cause we had an army on our tail for a lot of it."

"Well, hopefully we won't have that problem," Keairra said with a grin. "That's why we brought Trevor and his friends, after all."

"Exactly," Peym agreed.

Ξ

King Sladd was in his study entertaining two of his princes, Lykta and Lagereld, discussing their upcoming venture through the gateway to the jagtområder, when he felt it. Prince Spis was gone. The other two must have felt it as well, because their eyes widened and they looked at each other, then at him.

"My Liege?" Prince Lykta asked.

"Spis is dead," King Sladd said, standing up.

"Are you sure, my Leige?" Lykta asked. "Surely the lions don't have the ability to kill one of us!"

"Yes, I'm sure," King Sladd growled. "I was told that King Sværd lost two of his princes recently to an ambush by lions using some new form of magic. Until now I thought it was only a rumor being spread by his enemies.

"Lagereld, you are to take your forces and attack, immediately. Lykta, you are to prepare to go next."

Sladd turned to one of his guards. "Summon Eldstaden to my chambers at once, and send a runner to the main gateway. I need to know what happened."

"Yes, my Liege!" the guard said and left.

"May we take our leave, your Highness, to do as you have bid?" Prince Lykta asked; both he and

Lagereld were now prostrating themselves on the floor before him.

"Yes, go!"

King Sladd watched as they quickly left the room and wondered just what was going on? His own plans had been to not go through the main gateway until after it had grown to full size and stabilized. That time was still many duo-daers away.

He knew about Prince Talt's problems, the loss of one of his more powerful lords in single combat with one of those lions. King Sladd had been planning to use those problems against Prince Talt, taking him down a few notches until he was no longer a threat to Sladd's power, and perhaps even replacing him once this pass was complete.

Now this. Prince Spis had been one of his first princes and had been steadfastly loyal through all that time. Sladd had never had to replace him, or even consider it. With his loss, Sladd's power was significantly diminished. Raising up a new prince was not an easy process.

"You sent for me, my Liege?" Eldstaden asked as he entered the room.

"Yes, I did. Guards, leave us!"

Eldstaden stood there quietly as the guards quickly left the room.

"Prince Spis is dead," King Sladd said, getting directly to the point.

"And you have no one planned to raise up in his place, do you my Liege?" Eldstaden said. "Furthermore, this may embolden Prince Talt, as he has already replaced the lord he himself so recently lost."

King Sladd nodded. "You see the problem."

"Then I suggest you send Talt off to deal with the lord of the ley-lands. Properly presented, he will believe he is being granted a boon he can use against you later."

King Sladd nodded. "I have been having those same thoughts myself. But if he meets the fate for which we are hoping, then I will be down two princes. King Flik is likely to act on that advantage."

"Only if you have not found a new prince, my Liege."

"It will take many hundreds of daers to raise a new prince, you know that, Eldstaden."

Eldstaden nodded. "That is true, but if you are not here, then he cannot challenge you, can he?"

King Sladd sat back down on his throne. "So you also think I should go through to the jagtområder sooner, rather than later?"

"Yes, my Liege. It would allow you to gather a great deal of power quickly in case King Flik should get ambitious. Further, you might find yourself a new prince in those lands. With so much food running about, no doubt there will be an abundance of suitable candidates to be found among the feast?"

King Sladd thought about that. Normally he would wait until his princes and their lords had subdued the land and the prey before he showed up. Give them their heads and allow them to burn off the resentments that often festered between the hunts.

Perhaps Ansigt had been right, that a bold move was called for when faced with so much food. It only made sense to him that the fight would be harder, because the numbers as well as the rewards were so much greater.

Apparently great enough that even princes were having trouble prevailing. Obviously this feast of legend wasn't just meant for them to gorge themselves upon while growing fat and lazy. It was obviously meant to separate the weak from the strong. If he went through now, he could show them all how to deal with these lions and their ilk, and in the process of doing so, raise up princes of such power that he could kill Flik and take *his* princes away.

And after that, who knows? Did there really need to be so many kings and queens after all?

"Summon Talt to me. I want you to write up his task in such a way that he will believe we are unintentionally doing him the boon you suggested. Once he is gone, I will start preparations to take my house and my own lords into the jagtområder."

"As you wish, my Liege!"

Early Morning Washington

"Mr. President, we just received reports of a nuclear explosion ninety-two miles northeast of Reno."

The president yawned and, propping himself up in bed, he looked at the clock. It was a fair bit past five in the morning.

"Did you contact Sean?" he asked, looking back at the Secret Service agent.

"He's unavailable, Sir."

"What about his wife, err," the president fumbled a moment as he tried to remember which one was senior, "Rachel?"

"No one is available, Sir. General Baker is reaching out to his people there, but so far, no one seems to know anything."

The president sat up in bed, swung his legs over to the side, and put his feet on the floor.

"How big an explosion?"

"Approximately one kiloton, Sir."

"We don't have anything that small in our arsenal, do we?"

"I wouldn't know for sure, but no, I don't think so, Sir."

The president nodded slowly. "Okay. Call Mr. Bryson, and call director Kensington as well. Get Jill from homeland, and Baker from the Pentagon. Tell them we're having a meeting in thirty minutes; send out helicopters if you need to get them here on time."

"That soon, Sir?"

"Everyone in the world knows we're fighting a demon incursion in Reno. They're all watching it with their own satellites and whatever else they have. Right now I suspect every other head of state is also being woken up and told that we just set off a nuke.

"It would be nice if I had some answers for them when they start calling, don't you think so?"

"Yes, Sir! I'll get right on it, Sir!"

The president watched the agent run from the room and shook his head as he looked around for his slippers and tried to recall the man's name.

"Some days," he grumbled.

"You wanted to be president," his wife grumbled from the other side of the bed.

"That's true, that's very true. At least it hasn't been boring!"

Finding his slippers, he made his way to the shower. By the time he'd gotten dressed and strode into the Oval Office, there was a fresh pot of coffee sitting on the coffee table.

As he sat down at the head of the table in his favorite overstuffed chair, one of his aides handed him a cup of coffee, while another placed a plate with a cheese Danish on the small table on his left. Two much larger plates with pastries on them were set on the low table that sat between opposing couches. He was just finishing up his Danish when General Baker came in, looking quite crisp in his uniform. Jill from Homeland was on his heels; she didn't look as fresh, well groomed, or very awake yet, and grabbed a cup of coffee as she dropped down onto one of the couches to the right of the coffee table.

Director Kensington and Carl showed up next. Both looked considerably more awake, but Kensington was wearing slacks and a regular button-down shirt instead of his usual suit, while Carl was in jeans with a t-shirt.

The president turned to his chief of staff, who was wide-awake and dressed in a suit. Then again, he usually started his day at six, and it was now fifteen minutes after.

"Josh, where's Mister Bryson?"

"Still en route. They had to drive to a nearby field to meet the helicopter. They should be here in five, ten minutes tops."

"What happened?" Kensington asked.

"Someone, hopefully Sean, set off a large explosion to the north of Reno at the location of the demon's gateway," General Baker said.

"Did it destroy the gate?" Jill asked hopefully.

"No, it did not."

"Mores the pity," she said with a sigh and picked up a pastry.

"They've also launched a major counterattack against the demons there," General Baker said, continuing. "From what I've picked up so far, none of this was planned, it just happened. I'm unable to reach Sean's generals, or *any* of his leaders for that matter. It seems they're maintaining a communications blackout."

"There's been a development with the lions," Carl said, looking at his boss, who nodded as everyone turned to look at him.

"What kind of development?" the president asked.

"Apparently they came back."

"Came back?" Jill asked, looking confused.

"From what we've gathered," Kensington said, picking up the conversation, "most of the lions don't live on Earth; we're not even sure if they're actually 'alive'. They all live or exist someplace else. On another plane or something. We're not quite clear on that, and neither are the magic users. The lions haven't been forthcoming with any information on that either."

"Why am I not surprised?" Jill grumbled.

"They're gods, Madam Secretary," Carl said with an embarrassed look. "You can't expect them to tell us what they're up to."

"Anyway," Kensington spoke up again. "They're coming back. A lot of them, maybe all of them. Rumor puts it somewhere around thirty thousand of them have appeared in Reno and have been splitting up and traveling to where the other gates are."

"And this has what to do with this morning's explosion?"

"Explosion?" Carl said looking confused.

"Hello everyone! Good morning, Mr. President!" Steve said, walking into the room in his hybrid form, wearing a pair of shorts and nothing else. Tisha was right behind him, and was also in her hybrid form and similarly dressed. "Excuse our appearance. Now, as for that explosion, it's quite simple."

"Oh?"

"Sean and the lions are invading."

"Invading?" the president said, sitting up. "Invading what?"

"Why, the Onderwereld, of course," Steve said with an outrageous grin. "Seems they've had enough of these demons always coming here and messing up their home. So they've decided to do something about it, and they launched an attack through one of the gateways less than an hour ago."

The president noticed the shocked expressions on everyone's faces.

"Why weren't we told?" Jill asked.

"Because this is lion business, not human," Tisha said, and yawned, looking even more sleepy than Jill had when she showed up. "The explosion was simply a diversion," she added after her jaws snapped closed.

"Why weren't we told about the lions returning?" the president asked.

Steve put a hand on Tisha's arm, stopping her from making another curt response.

"Mr. President, you have to understand, the lions don't want anyone knowing how many of them there are, where they are, or even what they're up to. I don't understand the reasons for it, but that's just one of their many secrets. They didn't tell anyone they were coming back because they didn't want to cause a panic; they're not here looking to take over or run things. They're here to fight the demons and defend the Earth."

"Why?" Jill asked.

"Because we own it, it's ours," Tisha said with a smirk.

Steve gave Tisha a stern look and she blushed, causing several of the others to exchange a surprised glance.

"Look," Steve said before anyone could reply, "think of the lions as absentee landlords. They don't like to mess around much in human affairs because they like what we've done with the place. So they hang out at their favorite resort, work on their tans, and keep a few agents around to keep an eye on things.

"Suddenly a problem crops up with an invasive pest, one the tenants can't deal with, so they slap it down each time it becomes a problem. But this time, the pests come back stronger than ever, and suddenly they decide, rather than just keep slapping it down, they'll go to the source and deal with it.

"That's what's going on, to put it in more human terms."

"Steve, even *I* find that explanation to be condescending," Carl said.

"Well, if I let her explain it," Steve said with a nod towards Tisha, "you're all going to be a hell of a lot more insulted. Look," Steve said, grabbing Tisha's hand and dragging her around to the end of the couch on the left side of the table, which had the most open space, and dropped down into it, pulling her down next to him.

"I've discussed the whole thing with her, I've heard every story, every reason, and a lot of it just comes down to 'because we felt like it'. They're old; their leaders are even older. They take the long view, the several thousand years from *now* view.

"Well, Sean got pissed about having to deal with all this by himself, and he's young, so he *doesn't* take the long view. So he had words with his boss, and they had a big fight, and the end result is now they're all off helping Sean try to find a way to kill all the demons."

"They had a fight?" the president asked, looking shocked.

"Yup, real knock down drag out," Tisha said with a grin. "No one's punched Dad in the face in a real, *real* long time! Mom told me they really had it out."

"I hope Sean's okay?"

"He's fine," Steve said with a dismissive gesture. "But the point is, this sudden change in strategy is because Sean isn't willing to accept the number of deaths the lions were perfectly fine with, because they take the long view and Sean doesn't.

So in a few short days they decided to change the way they were doing everything."

"Besides which," Tisha said with another sleepy yawn, "we know they still have spies in the government, as well as other places. We didn't want anyone to find out what our plans were until after the fact."

"Still, it would have been nice to have been told in advance," the president told her.

"The blast was an unplanned diversion," Steve told them again. "Chad's taking advantage of the situation to push the demons back, for now."

"So this was another case of the 'wrath of the lions'?" Kensington asked.

Steve nodded. "Yes."

"Jim," the president asked, looking over at General Baker, "do we have any nuclear weapons that small?"

"No, we don't, Sir."

"Then we're left with the problem of what to tell the Russians, the Chinese, and even our own allies. I suspect there've already been more than a few requests about what happened this morning, Josh?"

The chief of staff nodded. "I think we've got at least two from every ally and major power now, Sir."

"Might as well tell them the truth," Tisha said with a shrug.

"I'm not sure they'll believe me," the president replied.

"With everything that's happened in the last year, I'm not sure that'll be a problem," Tisha said with a toothy grin.

"As long as we're here, Mr. President," Steve interrupted. "There is something else I want to discuss."

"That would be?"

"We're sending teams around to the other VA hospitals, and with the help of the Pentagon, we're tracking down many of the disabled vets."

"Yes, I know, Jim here has informed me of that, and we're all very grateful."

"Yes, well, I want to organize those people into a sort of 'home guard' and have them stand duty one day a week in their hometowns."

"Why?"

"Because we need someone who can quickly respond to any djevels that might make their way out here? We've got all these experienced soldiers who are now able to stand up and fight them. I'd rather not send them to the 'front', so to speak; they did their time, after all. But we could sure use them in the cities and the towns."

The president nodded. "I see your point. Jim?"

"I'll make it happen, Sir."

"Thank you. Now unless we have any other business, you're all dismissed. Oh, and before you go, I would appreciate it very much if any reports do come back from the lions who are invading the demons' home, they could find their way onto my desk?"

"I'll see what I can do, Mr. President," Steve said as he and Tisha got up, bowed, and quickly left the office.

"I don't think you're going to be getting any reports, Sir," General Baker said with a chuckle.

"What was that bit about them 'owning' the world?" Jill asked.

"It's true, they own it," Carl said with a lopsided grin.

"How can they own it? They got a bill of sale or something? I'd love to see them try and prove it belongs to them!"

"You're looking at this the wrong way, Ma'am," Josh spoke up, surprising everyone, as he'd been very quiet until now."

"And how's that?"

"They left their little paradise to come here and fight in a war because the planet belongs to them. However much you may find their claim to be ridiculous, I believe it bears pointing out that without them, we'd all be food by now."

"So in short, Jill," General Baker said with a laugh, "don't go looking a gift horse, or in this case lion, in the mouth."

Jill shook her head and sighed. "Okay, okay. Still, it rankles me a bit at times. They're all so young."

"Sean and Steve may be young," Kensington warned, "but don't forget that Tisha isn't. She's older than all of us. The same is true of their leader, whom she just told us is her father. From what I've gathered, speaking to Sean and Duncan, he's also a lot older than all of us."

"How much older?"

"I'm not sure anybody knows; it's kind of hard to believe someone could be over a hundred centuries old, it staggers the imagination. But recall that the elves and the dwarves have both said that when they got here, they found the lions already here."

"Okay, okay, I get it. Don't go pissing off the lions or they might start asking for back rent." Jill shook her head and looked around. "I wish I could call in sick and go back to bed."

#

"We need to find food," the First growled and dropped down onto his butt. They were all in animal form, as it made traveling a lot easier.

"Yes, food!" Peg grumbled from Sean's back, where she'd been riding for a while now.

Sean looked over at Estrella; neither of them were hungry.

"You want to know why they're getting hungry and we're not?" Estrella said to him.

"I'm surprised by it. I'd have thought we'd have lost whatever 'food' we'd gained when we went back home."

"Who cares?" the First said, looking over at the two of them. "The rest of us are hungry, and we better find food now before we're all starving like Peg is."

"The only way to get food is by killing djevels," Estrella warned.

"Fine, take us to a small town and let's wipe it out."

"All the towns here have a lord in them, who rules them and has several powerful demons that help him keep order in his town."

"Noted. Now how close is the nearest one?"

Estrella sat and pondered that a moment. They'd been walking at an easy pace for the last several hours, and she'd been making sure to avoid the towns she knew of. They were in Prince Spis' lands. He was a moderately powerful prince with a fair deal of lords, almost none of whom were extremely big. Spis had the most lords of any of the princes, but most of his were the least powerful.

Estrella had always found that an interesting approach. If Spis lost a lord, he didn't lose as much power as the others did, so the other princes quickly learned not to prey on his lords, because in a one to one exchange, he always came out ahead.

"We're in the northern part of Prince Spis' lands; he borders the mountains. I'm not intimately familiar with the area, but I think there's one off to the northeast, and another to the northwest of us. I'm not sure which is smaller."

"Pick the closer one, I'm hungry," the First grumbled.

"Okay, follow me then."

Getting back up, they all followed Estrella through the woods.

"I don't think I'll ever get used to these woods," Peym grumbled. "Black trees with black leaves just don't seem right."

"Hopefully we won't be here long enough that you have to," Libby agreed.

"In some ways it reminds me of my home, but not in others," Cali said as they walked.

"Oh?" Roxy asked. "How's that?"

"Well, home is very much dominated by blacks and whites. Many of the trees are covered in bark that is white, like your birch trees. Then there are those that are black, and of course in the winter the snows are all very white. But during the long nights of winter things get very dark, very black. The only colors you find in the winter during those long nights are inside the homes and the manors."

"Well, at least it's not all that cold here," Roxy said with a smile.

"Truly," Cali said, smiling back. "This place also seems to lack the peaceful feeling of the woods back home."

"You know, the First mentioned earlier that there is a lot of negative energy here. I wonder if that is from the djevels having lived here so long? If they corrupted it?"

"Might be a question to ask Mahkiyoc," Estrella mused from up front. "Now, no more talking, we should be drawing close to the edges of their fields soon."

"Saf'kij, Jipouet, scout and flank the right," the First said in a low voice. "Sasha and Nibisa, take the left."

All four lionesses quickly melted away into the dark trees.

Everyone else spread out into a skirmish line, Estrella at the center, with Sean on her left and the First on her right. They moved more carefully now as they picked their way closer, until suddenly they were just inside the woods, a cleared field lying before them.

The field was the same as the ones Sean had seen around Estrella's keep when he first came here. What they were growing, he still didn't know, as he'd never asked her about it, though she had mentioned it was some sort of food the djevels could eat.

Beyond the fields were the buildings. It didn't look so much like a town as a military installation. There was a low stone wall surrounding everything, and a keep that was probably twice the size of the one Estrella had lived in, having two large towers and a small building between them.

Laid out around the keep were a number of other structures. Sean wasn't sure what most of them were, but two were nice stone buildings that were probably about the size of a single-wide trailer. Everything else appeared to be made from the black wood the forests supplied, and while several of the structures weren't very large, probably half of them looked like longhouses.

Estrella looked back at them and spoke in a soft voice.

"Those small stone buildings are probably where the ridder or biskops live, or any magic users or special crafters, should they have one here. The long wooden ones are most likely the living quarters for gnashers and bonde. The higher-level demons will all live in the main keep, where they can serve the lord."

"What do they have in the way of weapons?" Keairra asked.

"Just swords and pole arms. If they have a magic user, they'll undoubtedly use it to cast spells, and of course the lord will have some magic as well, but this is a smaller keep, so he may not be very powerful."

"Everyone shift," the First said.

Letting Peg slide off his back, Sean shifted into his hybrid form.

"Ready your weapons. We'll start off with swords until we get into town. Don't use firearms unless you have to. We need to conserve ammunition."

Sean drew his sword from where it was slung over his back, next to his lever action rifle. He was also wearing two backpacks that were slung side by side. When he shifted into a lion they sat on his back like saddlebags. That was mainly because the fey armor prevented anything else from occupying the magical storage in their lycan collars. While some had complained about it, Sean pointed out that the weight limit of the collars would have prevented them from taking as much as they now had as well.

"I get the lord," the First said, continuing. "Make sure everyone gets at least a råge. I don't know if a bonde will be enough to feed one of us."

The First looked around and pointed forward with his sword.

"Let's go."

They came out of the woods at a trot. They were about halfway across the field when Sean noticed there were workers, gnashers, in the field, looking up at them in confused surprise.

Right up until Sasha and Nibisa swept in, still in their animal forms, and started killing them left and right, dispatching each with a swipe of a large paw. He noticed then that the other two lionesses were coming in from the other side doing the same thing.

"Just like the old days!" Keairra said with a laugh, and with that, they suddenly took off at a run. Sean let the others kill the handful of gnashers they ran down. It wasn't like he needed anything to 'eat', after all.

When they got in amongst the buildings, the fight turned serious. Bonde started pouring out of the buildings immediately. Some of them even had spears. Råge also showed up and were immediately set upon by five 'cubs', while the others slaughtered the bonde.

Sean noticed that while Roxy and Cali were giving a good account of themselves, Peg was hanging back. He guessed he shouldn't have been surprised; she wasn't much of a fighter, relying primarily on her skills with magic.

Spying a råge no one had picked up, Sean called out to her, "Follow me, Peg!" as he quickly fought his way over to the remaining råge. Sasha had joined them by now, and she helped keep any of the bonde from getting in his way as Sean slapped the råge in the side of the head, stunning it, then lopped off an arm and knocked it over, planting a foot on its chest and pinning it to the ground.

"Kill it, Peg! Quick, before it dies from its wounds!"

"Must I?" she asked looking at it a little worriedly.

"Do you want to starve?"

"Hell no!" Peg said and ran her sword through its head, killing it instantly.

"Hey! I felt that!"

"Great!"

"And I'm still hungry."

"Well, let's start cutting down the bonde and the gnashers. I'll stun 'em, you can kill 'em."

Peg nodded, but before they could get started, the demon lord came out. He was well armed and was even wearing a chest plate. The first thing he did was move to cast a spell, and Sean found himself dealing with that as the First quickly cut a path through to where the lord was standing.

"Lions? What are lions doing here!" the lord screamed and was then immediately fighting for his life. Apparently the First was *very* hungry.

Looking around, Sean saw there were two ridders and a biskop. Keairra quickly cut down the biskop, and Cali killed one of the ridders, while Peym got the other one.

Sean hit the lord with a magic missile, which stunned it for a brief moment, but that was all it took for the First to take its head off.

"Wives! With me! Let's clean out the keep. The rest of you, kill everything outside!"

Sean watched as all seven of the First's wives streamed into the keep behind him. Taking stock of the situation outside, Sean saw the others had things well in hand, so he stunned bonde and gnashers so Peg could kill them, killing a few of them himself in the process.

Several of the cubs found a raseri hiding in the other stone house, and Kalif killed it very quickly. Roxy also found another råge. So after that they all set to scouring the grounds, looking for bonde or gnashers, and anything else they could find.

When the First finally came back out of the keep, he looked pleased.

"We found a couple of mindre in there with another ridder. Estrella!" he called, looking around.

"Yes, Father?"

"We need to hit another town. We're still hungry."

"Sure, gather everyone up."

Five minutes later they were all back in animal form and loping off to the next keep Estrella knew about.

"How many of these do you think we'll have to hit?" Roxy asked.

Sean shook his head. "No idea. Stell?"

"Hell, I don't know, ask Dad! Prince Spis knows we're here now, we did just kill one of his lords."

"Well, we'd better hurry up and kill a few more before he comes looking for us, shouldn't we?" Keairra said, chuckling.

"Don't encourage him, Mother." Estrella sighed.

"Uh-huh. I'm still hungry. The lord at the next one is mine."

"Are we gonna have to kill a lord for each of you?"

"Well, that will depend on what else we find when we get there, now won't it?"

"Yes, Mother," Estrella sighed.

Ξ

Prince Talt was happy. At first he'd been worried about King Sladd's orders to go up onto the 'Mountain of the Dead' and investigate the truth of the old stories about the master of the ley-lines who once lived up there. It seemed King Sladd's own scribes' knowledge of the fabled permanent gateways was lacking, and it was believed by all that there were answers to be found up on the 'Mountain of the Dead'.

Prince Talt wasn't so sure about that. He'd heard the legends and the myths; all the princes and the lords had—that none who went up the mountain returned alive. But his own scribes couldn't name a single lord or prince who had met that fate. It was true that some bonde and even the occasional råge went up there seeking power, and of course were never seen again. But they were only bonde and råge, not anyone of any real power.

But for all that, Prince Talt was still happy. Because King Sladd's orders specifically allowed him to cut through the domain of the late Prince Spis. Prince Talt knew Prince Spis' death had hurt King Sladd deeply. Raising up a new prince would also take time, probably more time than Sladd could afford. But if his other princes were to gather up Spis' lords, Sladd would get that power back.

This whole trip was obviously just a cover for Prince Talt to do that. Apparently he still had his king's favor and that, along with the lords he would gather to himself on this trip, had left him feeling very happy. That and the three new lords he'd taken the vows of so far today. True, the lords of Prince Spis were not as strong, on average, as the ones Talt already had. Spis' tactic of many small lords was one that had caused as much anger as it had admiration in Prince Talt's mind. But with their prince now dead, they were all eager and willing to join themselves to him, because he was a powerful prince and they knew their own power would now grow, as he had promised to raise them all up to the level of his own lords.

"My Prince! We have a problem!"

Prince Talt looked up from his reverie. Hydda, the biskop who was the head of his guards, was riding back to him.

"What's wrong, Hydda?"

"The town, all of the beings there, all of them, are dead!"

"What?"

"Apparently there was a battle here some time ago, as even the former lord has disincorporated!"

Swearing, Prince Talt urged his mount onwards. "Show me!"

Thundering down the road a few minutes later Hydda led him into the town. Sure enough, there were the tar spots of the disincorporated everywhere. From the weapons laying beside them, as well as the gems and the armor in some cases, he could tell whoever had done this had been thorough.

"Watch my mount!" Prince Talt commanded and threw the reins to a bonde as he dismounted and strode quickly over to the open doors of the main keep.

At the bottom of the steps leading up to the doorway was a large spot of tar with the armor and sword one would expect of a lord. Swearing again, he strode up past the open doors and into the building.

It was carnage. Tar was everywhere, and while most of it was obviously just that of the gnasher and bonde servants you'd expect to find in a lord's keep, there were also several larger remains Prince Talt wasn't quite sure of.

"What do you make of it, my Prince?" Hydda asked when he came back outside.

"A large force came through here, harvesting and eating all."

"Do you think it was another prince? One seeking to deny you their oaths?"

Walking over to his mount, which was tearing chunks out of the dead bonde now under one of its feet as it fed quickly before it melted, Prince Talt shrugged.

"It may be, I cannot tell for sure. But I would expect any of my king's princes to be looking to consolidate, not destroy. It could be a party sent by King Flik to weaken our king further in preparation for a move against him."

Grabbing the saddle, Prince Talt pulled himself back up onto his mount, which was almost finished with its meal. This was quite unexpected, finding this kind of destruction so deep within the kingdom, and so close to his own lands.

"Let us continue on and see if the next town has also been destroyed."

"Yes, my Prince," Hydda said with a nod and passed orders down to the others to reorganize in preparation for marching on. Prince Talt watched as his men quickly gathered up the weapons and armor of the dead, as well as anything else of value they could find. That puzzled him the most. Who would kill so many and then simply leave such treasure behind?

Mountain Climbing

Sean was lying down with Cali and enjoying the afterglow of some truly wonderful sex. Apparently after she'd slain a biskop, she'd gained enough power to actually manifest a sexy looking set of bat-like wings on her back. They actually looked large enough to fly. She'd also gained a second smaller set on her head that were kind of sexy as well.

Sean had of course taken blatant advantage of the situation, not that Cali hadn't apparently been thinking the same thoughts.

"I wonder if I'll have these after we go back home?" Cali mused.

"I'd suspect not," Sean said, thinking about it. "They seem to be a creation of this place. In the lion world we're able to create all sorts of things, but none of them survive the transition to our world."

Cali sighed. "It would be nice to be able to learn to fly with my own wings."

Roxy shook her head. "For all that it looks good on you, I don't think it would be all that advisable for you to show up looking like a demon or a djevel when we get back home. People *might* get the wrong idea, after all."

"How much further, Estrella?" the First called out from the other side of camp.

"Two days."

"I thought it was two days when we started?"

"Might I remind *someone* that we detoured through how many towns in the last day and a half?"

The First snorted. "Blame your mother and your aunts."

"Five, we detoured through *five*. We're actually no closer now than when we started out."

"Well, I guess it's time to get up and head up the hill."

Getting up and stretching, Sean gathered up his armor as everyone else did the same, then checked to be sure his sword and rifle were slung. Then he checked the pouch he'd attached to his lycan collar, which had a few extra tags in it, as well as one of the silver bombs he'd had Daelyn make for him. Roxy was also carrying one, as were the First, Keairra, Dienna, and Sasha.

Last of all he slung the two large packs that had the ammunition for their rifles and pistols. For all that they had taken out five towns, they hadn't fired a shot yet. Each of the towns had been small enough that, combined with the element of surprise, they'd been able to easily overwhelm the forces in them.

"Are all of Spis' towns so small?" Roxy asked Estrella as they all started to move off.

"A lot of them are, but we're also on the outskirts of his domain. The forces around his castle, I've been told, were much larger and more powerful. Which is another reason we need to get moving. He'll know we've been killing his people, and he'll be sending out forces to engage us."

"No he won't," the First said as he came over to pad alongside Estrella. "He's dead."

"What? How do you know that?"

"Got it from that first lord I killed. The girls all got it too, from the ones they ate. Spis died back on Earth. I'm guessing Sean's diversion killed him."

"How can that be?"

"Adam, Roy, Scott, and Andre were all up in the forward command posts when the blast went off. Apparently Andre was close enough he got the Prince's soul when he died."

"He must have been pretty close," Sean said.

"Yeah, he said he got second and third degree burns over most of his body, even though he was in a pretty deep hole when it went off. None of the lycans who were with him survived, either." The First shook his head and sighed heavily. "I told him I didn't know whether to thank him or throttle him. I'm happy he destroyed the prince, but he shouldn't have gotten the others killed."

"It's hard for a lot of them," Keairra said, joining the conversation. "For so many thousands of years, back when we were young, we didn't care about whether any of them lived or died. We were immortal, we were gods, and they were all beneath us." She shrugged. "We're learning; those of us in the First Pride know the lives of the lycans have to be protected. The youngers…" she shook her head. "Some get it, some don't. Yet. They only know they're immortal once again. I fear there are some hard lessons ahead for some of our children."

"Especially if Sean gets his hands on them," Roxy said with a wink.

"Oh, he won't be the only one handing out lessons," Keairra said with a laugh. "Your father there really gets quite put out when he's not listened to."

"And then he makes us go straighten them out!" said Dienna, who had been listening nearby.

"Well, they are your children, after all," the First replied.

"Uh-huh. Like you weren't there when we made them!"

Sean just stayed out of the conversation and watched the byplay between the First and his wives as they walked along. He didn't recall them teasing each other this much back in the lion world. He wondered if this was because they were 'out' in the world again? Or was this just the kind of thing that went on when he wasn't around?

They'd been traveling for almost half the day when Rowan, who'd been detailed as one of the scouts to watch their rear, came trotting up, panting heavily.

"We're being followed," she told them.

"How is that possible?" Peg asked. "I thought their prince-guy was dead?"

Rowan shrugged. "They're way behind us; it took me a while to investigate, but they're back there, they're moving faster than us, and there's a lot of them. Big ones, too. I think a prince is leading them, and I counted almost a dozen biskops."

"Are you sure they're following us?" Estrella asked.

"They have a bunch of demons that look like dogs running at the front of them. They appear to be trailing us by scent."

"Well, no use in wondering why they're back there," the First said. "All that matters is they're there, and we'll have to deal with them. Let's keep an eye out for a place to ambush them and pick up the pace a little so they're not gaining on us."

"Do you think they know we're lions?" Sasha asked.

"If not, they're going to find out soon enough."

"Still no idea what our quarry is?" Prince Talt asked the råge in charge of the tracking demons.

"No, my Prince. The trackers do not recognize the scent, so I can only say it is something they've never run into before. But the scent is getting fresher, so we are gaining on them, my Prince."

Prince Talt turned to Hydda. "Get my guards ready for battle." He then turned to the two lords of his who were accompanying him on this trek. "Tvivel, you will take your troops and move to the left flank. Enkel, take yours and set up along the right. Once everyone is ready, we will move forward again."

"My Prince," Tvivel said, "aren't you worried about losing them?"

"I'm sure they know we're here now. I'd rather not walk into an ambush unprepared."

"Yes, my Prince!"

Prince Talt watched as they formed up. Neither Tvivel nor Enkel were his best; those he had sent to the main gate for the attack King Sladd was planning to avenge the loss of Prince Spis. But they were still both capable lords, and it didn't take them long to get situated. Once everyone was in their place, Prince Talt signaled to the råge in charge of their trackers to be off again.

For the next several hours, Prince Talt found his patience strained as he had to continually shout orders to either of his lords, and at times even his own guards, to keep the formation together and in good order. Moving this many demons through the dark woods was not an easy task, but he didn't care how hard their jobs were, as long as they did them. Tvivel and Enkel at least were being just as hard on their own bonde and the råge, ridders, and biskops ruling over them. Both knew that drawing their prince's ire would not bode well for their continued wellbeing.

"Damn, that's a lot of djevels," Sean said softly as he looked at the large group coming up the hill. There were eleven biskops, four on either flank, and each of those had the attendant ridder Sean had grown used to seeing. But the center formation had six ridder, two per biskop, plus six raseri and five mindre. There were also several raseri and mindre scattered among the two groups on the flanks, each of which was obviously being commanded by a lord.

Both of the flanking groups had hundreds of bonde and gnashers, possibly as many as a thousand each, and too many råge to count. The group in the center had only bonde, hundreds of them, and there were no gnashers to be seen. But they were being commanded by a prince.

"That would be Prince Talt," Estrella whispered back. "He is the most powerful of Sladd's princes. What he's doing out here is anybody's guess."

"Great, just great," Sean grumbled as he started casting a magical shield to cover all of them. They'd chosen this spot not just because the ground was favorable, but because a number of ley-lines joined here, and with the main gateway open, it was flush with power. Power Sean was tapping into to power up some serious spells. Peg was also tied into it, and was about to do some spells of her own to help them balance out the odds of the fight.

"So, eighteen versus three thousand, and they've got a prince and two lords."

"Ah! But we have repeating rifles!" Roxy said with a grin. "Can I shoot them now, *Dad*?"

"Fire!" the First growled, and with the sole exceptions of Sean and Peg, everyone opened up at once.

"The lords are shielded!" Roxy called out as her first shot was deflected. She immediately targeted a ridder, and was rewarded by it dropping out of the saddle of the beast it was riding. Which immediately stopped and started eating the ridder's still twitching body.

Cali had skipped the ridders and was targeting the råge, picking them off as fast as she could. She'd learned from both Estrella and experience that the bonde and the gnashers were an unruly lot and did not fight well without a strong hand at their back forcing them to. That was the råge's job in the djevel army, and she was determined to take as much of that link out as quickly as possible.

Estrella had started on the far-left flank and was targeting biskops. Her mother and two of her aunts were doing the same, starting at other places along the line. They'd discussed this among themselves while preparing. She'd hoped they'd be able to take out the lords; she doubted the prince would be going unshielded. But barring that, she thought going for the next rank down was a good place to start.

Sean was casting that magic missile spell he'd learned from the other lord. He spent several long seconds pumping it up with as much energy as he could leach out of the ley-line, and then he flung it out there, hundreds and hundreds of those nasty little self-homing missiles taking flight. Taking a moment to catch his breath, he noticed every gnasher that got hit dropped and didn't get back up. The bonde that got hit all dropped, but they didn't appear to be dead, while the råge that were hit slowed considerably. The rest of the demons on the receiving end looked annoyed mostly.

So he threw fireballs at the raseri and the mindres to try and take their minds off of attacking and make them think more about defending.

Peg looked around as the lions opened up on the djevels. The biggest problem with black powder was the smoke. There was a *lot* of it, and while it did make it hard for the enemy to see you after a few shots, it also made it hard for you to see the enemy.

On top of that, it made it pretty clear *where* the people shooting were, if the muzzle flashes and the noise weren't already giving you a clue. But she'd figured out a plan to deal with all that.

First was the smoke. She'd cast a wind spell that was blowing from behind them, pushing the cloud closer to the enemy, while helping to break it up. Second was a pair of illusions to either side of the djevel lines. She'd made a live copy of the lions doing the shooting and had cast it to those two flanking positions. Adding smoke and keeping it from being blown away took a little creativity and an artistic touch. While her phantom shooters might not be able to damage the djevels, it was helping to confuse them.

The First was picking his targets carefully with his single shot rifle, while keeping an eye on the situation before him. Their iron bullets were dropping the råge, bonde, and gnashers like flies. The larger demons, the raseri, ridders, biskops, and mindre weren't going down as easy. But they were going down.

The illusion spell Peg had cast was working well at confusing the djevels; their flanks were pulling in and turning to meet that threat. Once they moved forward and attacked it, they'd realize they'd been fooled. But until then, the numbers of those charging to attack them were being seriously diminished.

One of the mindre caught fire and started a small panic as the bonde around it tried to keep from being set on fire as well.

"The prince has shielded his remaining biskops and ridders!" Roxy called out.

"The lords are trying to do the same!" Sean called back and as the First watched, Sean launched all sorts of offensive spells at the lord on the right. He sent several fireballs, followed by something that looked like a spear that did what the fireballs could not and pierced the lord, making him reel in his saddle.

The First immediately fired at the lord, and it appeared Roxy was as well. Sean's next fireball caught it square on and set it on fire. It didn't last much longer after that, as the iron bullets quickly destroyed its head.

The First then watched as Sean repeated the attack on the other lord, but he had stopped trying to protect his people and had gone back to solely protecting himself.

Prince Talt couldn't believe what was happening! He was being ambushed from all three sides, and the weapons of the enemy were using that foul iron the lions had discovered! They needed to get closer; his demons had no ranged weapons, and sitting here, they were just being cut to ribbons. Lord Tvivel had already been cut down, and his more powerful demons were being slowly slaughtered as he watched.

"Charge!" Prince Talt screamed as loud as he could. "Engage the cowards! They cannot win if we engage them! Charge!"

Drawing his sword, he spurred his mount forward. If nothing else, it's snapping jaws would get his own people moving forward.

"Charge! Engage them!" he yelled again and gave a grim smile as he finally heard his biskops and ridders take up the call, followed by his råge as they spurred his bonde on.

Lord Enkel had also taken up the call and was pushing his people forward to attack one of the groups that was flanking them, while Lord Tvivel's people moved uncertainly. Those closest to his were moving forward with his own bonde, their råge now taking their orders from him. But others were moving to attack the flankers on their side, and even more milled around uncertain of what to do.

Prince Talt shook his head. He'd clean that mess up later, but right now he had a fight to win, before he lost too many of his own and had to abandon his task.

Another of those damnable magical missile spells flew out and took down the entire front line of his bonde. He'd lost at least a third of them; he had to close with this menace and destroy it while he still could!

Suddenly the fire coming from the ambushers changed. It went from what had sounded like the simple cracking noise he'd grown used to on the field of the hunting ground to a louder, more explosive sound, and small groups of the bonde up front were dropping with each explosion.

The change in tactics meant they must be close now!

"Attack! Attack! We have them now!" Prince Talt screamed, and just then a gust of wind blew the smoke past him and he could see who he was fighting.

It was a long line of lions. There were hundreds of them!

Peg smiled as she dropped the illusions to the sides of the fight, making it look like the ones fighting there had pulled back into the woods. Shifting her focus as the djevel prince and his demons drew near, she cast a mirroring spell to make it look like he now faced hundreds of lions instead of the baker's dozen it really was.

The effect was educational. The djevel prince froze in place, pulling up hard on the reins of his demonic mount, which must have picked up on his fear.

The bonde apparently didn't know what lions were, but the remaining råge did, as well as the three raseri, two biskops, and the one ridder of the prince's that remained alive.

Almost as one, all the lions roared then, and Peg's spell amplified it into a frightful sound. The two biskops and the single ridder wheeled their mounts around and rode past their petrified prince, who turned and joined them a moment later, with his remaining råge and the three raseri hot on his heels. The bonde, with no one to force them to fight, quickly fell apart, and didn't last much longer under the shotguns of the lions, who quickly dropped them and drew their swords to save ammunition.

Another mass of magical missiles shot out at the fleeing djevels, dropping all of the råge, as well as the mounts of the two biskops and the ridder.

Seeing their opportunity, two lionesses, Dienna and Sasha, jumped over the small embankment they'd been using for cover. Bulling their way past the bonde who were being slaughtered by the others, they charged after the three dumped djevels, who were squirming free of their dead mounts and trying to catch up with the others.

Tvivel's leaderless troops saw the slaughter and immediately turned and fled into the woods, running off in all directions.

Meanwhile Enkel had been moving his troops forward to support Prince Talt, as the attackers he'd gone after had fled. Seeing that his prince was in trouble, he turned his djevels again, leading them to cut across the back of Prince Talt's retreat to cut off any pursuit. It was just his unfortunate luck to come across two lionesses who had just finished administering the coup de grace to a pair of biskops with their shotguns.

He never even saw the huge lion who got him by the throat, as the First, seeing two of his wives being attacked by a lord with an army following him, lost any and all semblance of civilization and showed everyone what he was truly capable of when he was pissed.

Enkel's forces watched as the biggest lion they'd ever seen grabbed their lord by the neck and knocking him out of the saddle, then began shaking him viciously. They then noticed that their prince was fleeing with a number of lions in hot pursuit as the First's other wives joined the battle, along with their children. So they did the only sensible thing they could.

They fled after him.

"Damn, he got away," the First growled as he dropped the dead lord on the ground. Keairra had ripped the head of the lord's mount off when it had tried to bite him.

"And what did you two think you were doing?" The First sighed, looking over at Dienna and Sasha.

"Playing cleanup, what else?" Sasha said with a saucy grin.

"You know you could have been hurt!" the First growled at them.

"Nah, we knew you'd watch out for us!" Sasha said, and coming over, she dropped to her knees and gave him a hug. "Thanks, Sot."

Dienna came over and hugged him too. "Yes, thanks, Kame, for watching over us."

The First tried to growl at them again, but his heart wasn't in it.

"I'm such a sucker for you two," he grumbled.

"Oh, you're a sucker for all of us!" Keairra laughed. "That's why we put up with you!"

"So now what?" Sean asked, coming over to the First and the Pride, all of whom were standing around him.

"I guess we continue on to that blockhouse Mahkiyoc is in. There's a lot fewer of them now than there were when they attacked, so I don't think we'll be seeing them again."

Estrella shook her head. "I just wonder what they were doing here. This is way out of Prince Talt's realm."

"Maybe he was grabbing Spis' lords now that Spis is dead?" Sean suggested. "Then when he found the towns we'd wiped out, he came to investigate?"

"Doesn't matter," the First said. "We won, they lost, and ran off with their tails between their legs. By the time anyone comes back, we'll be long gone. So let's get our stuff together and get a move on."

Sean nodded. "Sure thing, Dad."

Retrenching

It took Prince Talt half of a daer to gather up his forces. Almost half of Tvivel's were still missing, no doubt still running home. Enkel's forces were in much better shape, having joined his retreat as their lord died. In fact, three of Enkel's biskops had survived, as well as two of his ridders.

All five of them were prostrated before him now in his command tent.

"As you all know, your lord died in valiant service to me, defending my flank after my own officers were killed. I hope his successor shows as much strength and courage as he did."

"I beg your pardon, my Prince," one of the biskops said, "but which of us do you intend to raise up to his place?"

Prince Talt smiled and stood. "That question I will leave to the five of you to debate. The winner can find me when you're done, and I will take the oath. Guards!" The dozen demons that now made up his guard suddenly stood to attention.

"Come with me; let us leave them to work this out in private!"

The last guard had barely stepped out of the tent when the sounds of fighting broke out from inside.

"Half of you stay here, the other half come with me," Prince Talt said as he headed off towards where Tvivel's survivors were gathered. Only one of Tvivel's biskops had survived, or at least come back to him. He was going to bind that one to him next. He regretted setting Enkel's survivors against each other, but he couldn't afford to have any biskops around that weren't sworn to him after the day's failure. He could not afford for word of this to reach King Sladd. The damage to his reputation and his standing could be fatal.

"My Prince!" the biskop said and prostrated himself as Prince Talt walked up to him.

"What is your name, biskop?"

"Höger, my leige!"

"Are you prepared, Höger, to swear the oath of a lord and bind your self to my crown?"

"Yes, my Prince!" Höger replied enthusiastically.

"Good, then let us begin..."

Prince Talt had been finishing up with Höger when a wounded, but still alive biskop was brought before him by his guards. The winner of the fight in the tent, and he still had his ridder with him as well. The loyalty of the ridder to his biskop impressed Prince Talt, and he elevated him to biskop after he'd sworn in his new lord, Lord Makt. He then gave the new biskop his surviving two raseri to eat, so he might make the physical transformation to his new station.

Prince Talt had planned on eating those two himself, just as he had already eaten the other survivor. He had little tolerance for cowardice in the face of the enemy,lion or not. But rewarding loyalty was important, especially after the day's events.

"What are your wishes, my Prince?" Lord Höger asked as they watched the ridder cheerfully consuming his reward.

"We will go back to Spis' lands and sweep up as many more of his lords as possible. We need to build up our numbers and replace our losses if we are going to deal with such a large number of invaders."

Both of his new lords bowed their heads at that.

"You will not speak of what happened with anyone. You will instruct your followers not to talk of this as well. We survived a fearsome ambush meant to take on far greater numbers than we were. I do not want the rank and file to believe that this was anything other than what it was: a strategic retreat so we may come back in greater numbers to crush our foe."

"Yes, my Prince," both lords said, bowing before him.

"Now, see to your troops. After everyone has rested, we will get started."

"Yes, my Prince," they both said, and after bowing a second time, they took their leave.

Prince Talt reflected that the only person here that was still alive that knew of his original orders to go up the 'Mountain of the Dead' was himself. Hydda, the head of his guard, was dead, as was the rest of his personal guard, and the two lords. If any of the survivors should be questioned by King Sladd, they would only hear that he had been investigating the destruction of Spis' lords, and come across an army of lions.

Upon hearing that, he could only hope King Sladd would forget about the original order he had given him.

Still, it wasn't something Prince Talt wanted to put much credence on. It looked like King Sladd was starting to suspect his plans, and if that were the case, any excuse for King Sladd to be rid of him would be quickly seized and used.

So he would do as he told his two new lords. He would sweep through more of the dead prince's lands and gather up as many more lords as he could over the next several daers. He would stop by the ones he'd already coopted as well and gather up some of their gnashers and bonde to replace those he'd lost.

Then he would send a messager to the king, while he himself went after these lions in force. By then, his loss would either be forgotten or overlooked in the panic the knowledge that lions were here would bring. Because he had to keep sight of what was the most important thing in all of this: His life.

Ξ

"Why are we retreating again?" Mayor Schiere asked.

"Because Chad said so," Adam told her as he tried to withhold a sigh. With Sean gone, the weekly, or now *bi-weekly*, meetings with the mayor and city council had fallen to him. He really didn't want to do it, but Daelyn had told him after Sean, he was the only lion around here everyone knew, and he was forced to admit she was right.

Namely by that big nasty hammer she had. Sean had warned him she wouldn't hesitate to brain Adam with it, because she'd already brained *him* with it. More than once.

"Chad?"

"Our head military officer," Daelyn supplied. That she had to suffer through this along with him made him feel a little better.

"And why is he retreating?" one of the city council members asked. "Wouldn't it be better to keep attacking them and keep them away from the city?"

"No, actually." Adam said. This was something even he understood. "You see, we no longer have fortifications or support outside the city perimeter. We moved everything we could back to the city, and the djevels destroyed anything of value we left behind. The counterattack we launched on them was solely to take advantage of circumstances and bleed them a little.

"But they're already coming back, and they're coming back in even larger numbers this time than they did before. So trying to fight them on the open field is a fight that favors them and their large numbers."

"And favoring them is not how ya' win a war," Daelyn added.

"So Chad pulls back inside our perimeter, and we fight on our terms."

"But won't that just make it easier for them to take the city?" another council member asked. "We all thought when you pushed them back, that the city was safe now!"

"It's going to be a long time until any of us are *safe*," Adam growled. "A bit more than two and a half years. As for the city, we need you to get back to work on the evacuation plans."

"If you want us to work on evacuation plans, why are we still building defenses?"

"To slow them down, obviously," Adam said, and this time he did sigh. "And who knows? Maybe we'll get lucky and be able to keep them out. Look, you all need to understand that Sean is a much nicer and more reasonable person than I am. So let's not make me explain things over and over again. Just accept it and move on so I don't lose my temper again."

"What do you mean 'again'?" the mayor asked.

"He's the lion wot killed tha' colonel at the airbase," Daelyn supplied helpfully. "Twisted his head right off I believe?"

Adam grinned, showing all his teeth, which had something of an effect on the people in the room, as he was in his hybrid form. Roxy's dad would probably give him shit later over it, but compared to Roxy, her father was downright reasonable.

Plus he was off briefing the governor today.

"Umm, yes. I see," said the mayor, shuffling the papers on her desk. "Robert, get everyone working on that plan again. I expect to see a draft on my desk by lunchtime *tomorrow*. Understand?"

"Yes, Mayor," the councilman who had been balking said with a resigned sigh.

"And when did you say Sean will be back?" the mayor asked Adam.

"When he's done, of course. Now, can we review the progress on the I-80 barricade?"

"I thought we were going to stop them at McCarran?" asked Kelly, the replacement for Josh.

"If you've ever taken the time ta look at castles and their walls, there is always a second one behind the first, an even a third line of defense," Daelyn said, in the kind of patient voice parents used to explain things to especially dim-witted children.

"Oh," Kelly said and looked a little embarrassed. "You'll have to forgive me. This isn't the kind of thing I'm used to."

"Well, you've been doing a great job," Adam said soothingly. "So don't worry your head too much. But we do need to use this time to get those defenses prepared, so if they make it past McCarran, we can stop them there."

Adam smiled as Kelly nodded and pulled out a number of rolled up engineering drawings. Maitland had given him a list of things that were concerning him, and Adam was going to make sure all of it was addressed before they left today.

"I thought I was going to have to sit on you back there!" Adam laughed as Daelyn and he got into her car.

"Earth and stone! Those people are so damn annoying! No wonder Stell and Cali killed one of 'em. Maybe they shouldn't have stopped with just the one!"

"Now you know why I didn't bring Ryla," Adam said, still laughing. "She would have beaten the town council half to death." Adam paused a moment. "Or beaten half the council all the way to death!" He snickered then. "Man, I love that woman. Let's go find Chad, he's up at the McCarran command post."

"I'm shocked they dinna ask about the explosion."

Adam shrugged. "To them, they're all the same. Plus it was a couple of days ago. I doubt they've even put it and Sean's departure together."

"None 'a the lycans on their staff told 'em?"

"Nope, Sean, me and the First ordered everyone not to talk about it to the mundanes."

Daelyn thought about that and changed the subject.

"Ya know, I've heard ya say that the First ain't ya father, that Stell is just a half-sister."

"Yup. And?"

"So just who is ya father? Anyone I know?"

Adam nodded. "Sampson's my dad."

Adam bounced off the door as Daelyn made a sudden correction. Adam's revelation had apparently distracted her from driving for a moment.

"Sampson's ya dad?" Daelyn said with a touch of disbelief in her voice.

"Didn't I just say that?"

"Does Sean know?"

"Maybe? I don't know? I think I mentioned it to him a while back, I don't remember."

"Wow. What's he think about ya Ryla?"

"They don't like each other. I think she might have put the moves on him once long ago when she was young and dumb."

"Must be rough."

"Not really, Dad and I haven't gotten along for over a thousand years. Though Mom tells me he's really proud of what I've been doing here."

"What, ya haven't asked him?"

Adam snorted. "I haven't talked to him since he came back."

"You haven't talked to ya own father!" Daelyn said, shocked.

"I didn't want to interrupt him; he's been pretty seriously shacked up with Sean's mom since he got back, you know." Adam stopped a moment and then laughed again. "You know, I guess this is gonna make Sean my step-brother as well as my brother-in-law."

Daelyn gave an evil snicker. "Anna his step-son as well."

"Oh? How do you figure?"

"Well, you're Sarah's half-brother now, right?"

Adam started to laugh even louder. "Oh my, can you imagine the look on Sean's face when I call him 'Dad'?"

Daelyn couldn't help but laugh with him at that. "Don't forget to call Rob 'Mom'! I'm sure that'll set her off!"

"Oh! What about Rox?"

"You do that, and make sure I got me camera first, because I want to record it as she beats you to death!"

"You know, it just might be worth it!" Adam said, still snickering as Daelyn pulled up in front of the command post.

"You might as well head back home to the kids," Adam said as he opened the door to get out. "I suspect I'm gonna be here for the rest of the day."

"Sure. I'll let Ryla know."

"Later, Dae!" Adam said and, closing the door, he walked over to the door of the command post as Daelyn took off in a shower of gravel and noise.

"Hi, Adam," Chad said, looking up from his plot board as Adam came in and closed the door behind him.

"How goes the war?"

"Not great, but as expected," Chad said, motioning to the map and markers before him. "They're pushing us back, not that we're giving them much resistance. Our long-range reconnaissance is showing us that a *lot* of djevels are coming through the gate now."

"Cali's not here; you *can* call them demons, you know."

"Eh, I like djevels. The word 'demons' makes people think we can't beat them. It makes 'em sound scarier. Djevels is different enough from demons that people don't fear it as much."

"Huh, hadn't thought about that."

"War is about a lot more than just the physical."

"So how long before you think we're bottled up in Reno again?"

"Probably by midnight. Thank god for lycans' natural night-vision. It definitely took the advantage of nighttime away from them."

"And now the question no one's been asking: How many random mobs are out there moving off to attack cities?"

"Oh, less than a handful, I'm sure," Chad replied.

"Really?"

"Yup. All the mobs heading off to Salt Lake City, Sacramento, and points north aren't random at all. They're very well put together now."

"So what are you going to do about them?"

"You been talking to Sean?" Chad asked, looking at Adam accusingly.

"Not yet, but I have a pretty good idea what he's going to ask, and I do *not* want to tell him I don't have any answers."

Chad nodded and went back to looking at his maps. "Point. We're going to bomb them with some special munitions some air force group is working up. Iron frag bombs. I don't think we'll be able to stop them all, but Maitland and I are hoping to put enough of a dent in their numbers that the other cities will be able to stand against them."

"Why aren't we using those bombs here?"

"Because we want to draw them here where we can deal with them?" Chad replied. "Everyone is hoping Sean comes back with some sort of nasty weapon we can use. Until then, I'm going to keep using my lion infantry every chance I get to try and whittle their numbers down."

Adam nodded. "Well, I'm gonna gear up and go join the troops."

"It's going to be a long time before they get here, Adam."

"Yup, and morale out there isn't going to build itself. With Sean off invading the Onderwereld, I need to go out there and get some face time."

"You know," Chad said, looking up with a smile, "with Sean gone..."

"I'll think about it." Adam smiled back. "But! You won't be in the first few groups. Generals don't lead from the front, except in bad Hollywood movies."

"Why, thank you, Adam."

"Don't thank me yet, I still haven't said yes!" Adam said and went out to find his team. He was already armored and had his sword. All he needed now was to track down a rifle and some ammunition.

Ξ

"My King," Eldstaden said, coming into King Sladd's chambers. "You have summoned me?"

"Yes. Prince Lagereld sent a messenger that I received just this morning. Someone has killed one of his lords along the border with Prince Skarm. He was rightly incensed, but as Skarm is through the gateway, I have no idea who the guilty party in this affair is. I would have you look into it. Fighting during a pass is forbidden, and I would know who is causing me these problems."

"I will start my investigation immediately, my King."

"Thank you, Eldstaden. Have you any word on Prince Talt?"

"No, my King. Not a one. I take it he is still alive then?"

"Yes, very. His power has been increasing, slowly, so think he's taking advantage of the dead prince's lands and binding the lords there to himself."

"Well, you figured he would do that, did you not?"

"Some, yes, but I thought he'd have more sense than to delay this long on the mission I've sent him on. I'm thinking of sending Prince Vises Ikke into his lands to take his lords away from him now, instead of waiting until after he's dead. I'm starting to find him annoying. He should either be dead or returning here to tell us what he's learned."

"Have you decided to kill him then, My King?"

King Sladd shook his head slowly. "As much as he annoys me, I am already down one prince; I'd rather not be down a second one just yet. Assuming he survives his mission to the mountain, I'm considering putting him in charge of the slave pens. Someone will need to be here to see that the food is protected long enough for a permanent link to be created, after all."

"Have you given any thought to our earlier discussion?"

"Yes, Eldstaden, I have been thinking about it, and I have decided I will be going through the gateway early. After Prince Lagereld has joined his forces with those of Prince Skarm, I will summon my lords and order them to prepare."

"All of them, my King?" Eldstaden asked with a concerned look.

"Yes, all of them. I've ordered Skarm and Lagereld to take the town to the south of the gate. I will immediately move there, make it my castle, and deploy my lords around it to fortify my position. I will then give Skarm and Lagereld their heads to do whatever they please, while I assign Prince Lykta to round up as much food as he can and move it back here."

"What of Prince Vises Ikke?"

"If Talt dies, I'll give him Talt's assignment with the pens. Otherwise I will have him maintain my presence here until I decide my next move. I want to see what Princes Skarm and Lagereld can accomplish before I decide on rotations and assignments."

"Wise, my King."

"I see the challenges of this jagtområder will be many, but I do not believe they will slow us down for much longer. We have always prevailed; we *will* always prevail."

#

"Well, Jesse, what do you think?" Trevor asked his second in command as they looked down onto the fairly large demon village. This one actually appeared to have workshops of some sort, and a lot more larger buildings than the one they'd hit on the first day they'd come here.

Jesse growled at him, "I think if you don't let us go down there and eat, you're going to be facing quite the uprising."

"Everyone knows better than to hit towns that are too close together. That'll make it easier for them to find us."

"That may be, but everyone is starving, too. I think we've about hit our limit. We don't go down there soon, and we're going to stop being effective."

"We hit that town, and we're not going to get everyone. Some of those djevels are going to get away."

"Well, how can we have a reign of terror if they don't know we're terrorizing them?" Jesse grumbled back at him.

Trevor laughed and then smiled at her. They'd been mates once and had several cubs. He'd specifically asked for her because he trusted her opinions. "Yeah, good point. Let's get everyone ready and go kill stuff. Least with a town this big we should all be able to eat well."

Walking back towards the others, Trevor waved them all closer.

"Okay, Jesse is going to take half of you and circle around to the other side, while we get ready up here. I'll leave it up to you, Jess, to decide when to attack. Once you've got them focused on you, we'll charge in from up here and see how many we can take from behind.

"Lead off with your rifles, and mind where you're throwing any grenades! We want to take down the big guys, because they'll feed everyone the best. Also it'll fuck 'em all up the most as well. We're not gonna get everyone, so don't even try. If they're running away, let 'em go unless they're worth eating.

"And make sure you don't go running off alone! Understand? Yeah, you're hungry. I'm hungry, we're all hungry!"

"So let's eat!" Jake yelled from the back.

"Ha, ha, Jake. Funny. The point is, let's not get into a feeding frenzy. We're not a bunch of damn fish. There's a lot more of them down there than there are of us, so keep your heads together. Got it?"

Everyone nodded.

"Jesse, take your team and go. The rest of you, let's set up on the hill and get ready."

"Later, Trevor!" Jesse said with a smile and, gathering up twenty of the others, she took off at a trot through the strange black trees that seemed to be everywhere.

Spreading out, they moved to the edge of the tree line and settled down to wait.

"How long do you think she'll take to get there?" Lena asked in a whisper.

"This is Jesse we're talking about, and she's hungry," Trevor said and chuckled. "Thirty seconds?"

Trevor wasn't sure exactly when Jesse did attack because she was out of sight due to the buildings, but the moment all the demons started to run around, he figured it could only be her.

"Alright, everyone! Let's go! And don't do anything stupid! We're gonna be here for a while!"

Drawing his shotgun, Trevor led the charge down into the town. The others could go for picking things off at a distance. He wanted his demons up close and personal when he killed them so he could feed. This whole place was just bizarre beyond belief, from the black sun to the black trees. From eating things by just being close to them when you killed them, to the whole lack of any real biological functions.

He hadn't had a drink of anything in days, and wasn't thirsty.

That just wasn't right.

Bypassing a couple of gnashers, he ran right up to a råge and shot it in the head, enjoying the sudden lessening of his hunger. But all things being equal, he'd rather be eating a steak, or even just killing and eating rabbits in a field somewhere. This was just... unnatural.

Moving into the town, he saw Jesse's group at the other end of the wide dirt road that went through the middle of it all, and there were a *lot* of demons there, even a lord! Aiming for a biskop that hadn't noticed them yet, Trevor charged forward, switching the shotgun to his left hand as he pulled his pistol with his right.

He was definitely going to eat his fill today.

"Damn, that was weird!" Jake said as they sat down to take a break. "I mean, you eat, and you expect to feel full at some point. But hell, all I felt was less and less hungry until I wasn't hungry anymore. After that, anything I killed I didn't feel anything anymore!"

"Yeah, Esti told me Sean killed so many of them with that bomb of his that he probably won't have to eat for a hundred years. But if a demon gets too much food, they transform into something bigger and badder."

"Like Pokémon?" Jake asked with a grin.

Grism, who was sitting next to Jake smacked him one.

"Thanks, Grism," Trevor said, laughing.

"Him and that damn game!" Grism grumbled. "If I ever find out who brought it back..."

Trevor grinned and shook his head. Some lions had damn near photographic memories and made a killing in trading favors by creating modern things in the dream world when they slept each night. The card game fad had ripped through the entire lion world almost overnight until the next fad caught up with them. But there were still more than a few hardcore players. Grism was one, and Jake teased him about it constantly.

"So what's next, Sweetie?" Jesse asked Trevor as she leaned heavily against him.

"Looks like somebody wants something," Lena chuckled from where she was lying next to Tad.

"Well, I was thinking we should move further away from here, but not until after we've all had a nice little break," Trevor said and, leaning back against Jesse, gave her a kiss. "Then after a few days of travel, look for another place to attack."

"And then?"

"And then we do it all over again until the First tells us to go home."

"It's going to be different having everyone alive again," Jesse said with a happy smile. "Almost like old times."

"You just want to be able to have kids again!" Jake teased.

"Yup, and I got my favorite daddy right here next to me!"

"You know there aren't any lion souls waiting to be born, Jesse."

Jesse nodded. "Time to make some new ones then, isn't it?"

Trevor put an arm around her and pulled her into a hug. "You know what? I like the sound of that. But! We're not making any in this place, this place is just fucked. Let's wait until we get home."

"Yes, let's."

Truth & Rights

Estrella stopped as they got to the tree line.

"Why are we stopping?" the First asked.

"Because we're about to step out into the open. If you look all the way up there, you can see the blockhouse we're heading for."

"So everybody, check your gear and let's not look threatening," Sean said, then immediately turned to look at Cali, who was thankfully looking like her usual self.

"I figured out this morning that looking like a djevel was probably not a good idea, my Husband," she said with a smile.

Sean breathed a sigh of relief.

"That's why I stopped," Estrella admitted. "I also think it would probably be best for Cali to be in the center of us. Sean and I will go first; hopefully he'll recognize us."

"I have a better idea," the First said. "Why don't the two of you go up there alone, and after he's let you in, you can tell him about us. Once he's okay with it, you can come back to get us."

Sean looked at Estrella, who shrugged. "Okay, I guess."

Sean nodded. "Well, let's go see if we're still welcome here or not."

Leaving the cover of the trees, Sean and Estrella slowly walked up to the metal door, the same as they had before. He wondered briefly how many months ago that had been. Things had been happening so fast he hadn't the slightest idea. He had his mana shield up now, because with the main gateway open, the ley-lines up here tried to overload him with mana every time he stepped on one. Thankfully he'd taught Peg the spell as well, as she'd been having the same problem.

"What manner of demon be you?" a disembodied voice asked.

"Mahkiyoc Aan Drues, it's Sean and Estrella. We were here many duo-daers ago, before the main gateway opened. Don't you remember us?" Sean asked, a little worried.

"Sean and Estrella... Oh, you are those two lions. I remember now. You said you would come back with your friends, and here you are. Is that them waiting back by the trees?"

"Yes!" Sean said with a nod. "Several of the females are not lions, but they are with us as well."

"The machines had noticed, it thought one might be a demon. Are you sure they're not?"

"Yes, I'm sure."

"Come inside first so that we may talk."

The door opened then, and looking at Estrella, Sean shrugged and stepped inside with her following.

As the door closed behind him, Sean walked down the hallway to the other end. The walls of the entire hallway were alive with a shocking amount of power now. He would be very interested to see what he could do with so much power once they were settled in.

The other doorway opened when they got to the far end of the hallway, and Sean went upstairs to where they had met Mahkiyoc when they were here last.

As before, the stairway let out into the back of a large room, which had a nice-looking white carpet on the floor. The walls were covered in a combination of screens that appeared to show the outside world, and artwork, some of which contained colors other than the never-ending black and grey that seemed to consume this world.

The same tables and furniture were set out around the room; it still looked very much like a large living room, unchanged from their last visit. At the far end, the long window that dominated the far wall still looked outside, with the large consoles with seats still before them. Mahkiyoc still sat behind the one console that faced towards the stairs and seemed unchanged from when they had last seen him, still appearing to be a man in a white robe with long gray hair and gray-tinged skin.

"You'll have to excuse me," Mahkiyoc said as they came into the room. "I have been so busy with my research that everything else has been pushed to the back of my mind. It wasn't until you said my name that I realized I must have met you before and searched my memories."

"Why did you want to bring us up first?" Estrella asked.

"Oh, to be sure you weren't in thrall to any demons. I am the last of my people now, so that carries a certain amount of responsibility. So what is the story with the dark female?"

"She's a dark elf. They live very close to one of the negative planes. They make a sport of killing demons, apparently. They like them even less than we do."

"If such a thing is possible," Sean added.

"Fine, I will invite them up. Why did you come back?"

"Because you asked me to, and I told you I would," Sean said. "And I told you I would bring my friends so we could see if we could use those old weapons you mentioned against the demons."

"Oh! I was wondering why I was researching those old things. Now I'll just have to find the file I put together. It's here somewhere."

Mahkiyoc touched something and, turning to look out the window, said, "You may come up and join your friends. The door is open, and will close once all of you are inside."

Mahkiyoc looked back up at Sean. "This will be most interesting. I will finally be able to cross-reference observations from natives on another plane to the ones I've made here. This should greatly improve my research."

"If you can show us how to make those weapons and use them, we might be able to rid this world of demons."

"Oh, I don't think there are enough of you for that!" Mahkiyoc said with what Sean guessed passed for a chuckle.

"There are many more of us here already, and if necessary we will bring in reinforcements, but I'm not our leader. I'll introduce you to him once they've come upstairs."

Sean left Estrella to talk to him as he went back down to the entryway. It wasn't all that long before the door opened, and everyone stepped into the large foyer.

"Dad, I need to introduce you to Mahkiyoc."

The First nodded and followed Sean up the stairs, with all of his wives coming along as well.

"You'll have to show my husband," Estrella was saying. "He understands technology; I'm still learning."

Sean led the First over; he'd ask Estrella about whatever it was later.

"Mahkiyoc, this is our leader, he is known as 'The First'."

Mahkiyoc looked the First over. "You feel very much like Omushkego Aan Creus. More so than the one called Sean."

"Yes, he did something to me and my Pride a very long time ago. We only remember it because he was killed by what we later learned was a demon, which we then killed."

"While I mourn the senseless loss of my cousin, I must recognize his success. I have thought on what the one called Sean and the one called Estrella asked, and I do think you have enough of Omushkego Aan Creus' essence inside you to be able to use our machines."

"Sean told us you might have weapons we could use against the demons in our war against them?"

"Yes. I have found the information. The machines with which we made them may still work."

The First considered that a moment. "Also, you mentioned to Sean that there is a machine we could use to lock the gates to our world so the demons could no longer go there?"

"There is such a machine; it occupies a place much like this one. However, I do not know if it still works. Nor am I sure I could use it. I am a researcher, not an engineer."

"Can you show us where it is, and how to get there?"

Mahkiyoc pondered that a moment before answering.

"You would have to learn how to use our machines first, assuming that is possible. I would much rather spend my time talking to you about your world and comparing my observations to yours, so I may increase my knowledge."

The First nodded. "I would welcome a long discussion with someone older and wiser than myself. As the oldest among us, I would be honored to talk with you, as long as during those times when I must sleep you were to teach my family here how to use your machines."

"It will take much time to teach them," Mahkiyoc pointed out.

"Time is something we have much of, is it not?"

"A strong point," Mahkiyoc said and looked thoughtful for a moment. "It is agreed. Now, let us begin."

The First turned to Sean. "Could you get everyone settled, Son? It will be a while before I must sleep."

Sean nodded and gestured to Keairra and the rest, who followed him back downstairs.

"I'm surprised he didn't want to know any of our names," Dienna said.

"Either his society was strange, or he's lost all social skills after being alone for like a million years," Estrella said.

"Come on, let me show you to your rooms," Sean said, motioning to the others.

"Where do those stairs go?" Kalif asked.

Sean shrugged. "Beats me, we didn't have the time to explore when we were here last."

"Well, I'm claiming the room we had last time," Estrella said while grabbing Roxy, Peg, and Cali. "Don't take too long, Sean!"

It only took Sean a few minutes to show the others where the other rooms were, then he joined his wives.

"I can't believe the amount of power in this place!" Peg said as Sean closed the door behind him.

"It's basically a giant mana battery," Sean agreed. "I thought it was big before, but it's got more of a charge in it now than it had last time."

"What do they use it for?" Roxy asked.

"They've harnessed it to run all their machines, apparently."

"The same machines that open all the gates?" Peg asked with a thoughtful look.

"I guess, why?"

"Makes you wonder if the reason they open the gates is to fill their batteries..."

"... so they can open more gates," Roxy finished.

"He said the gates were a natural phenomenon," Sean pointed out.

Estrella shook her head. "He told us they modified the natural gates so they would open where they wanted them to. That's not exactly the same thing."

Sean thought about that, as well as Peg's unasked question. What would happen if they drained all the batteries? Would the gateways to their world stop functioning? Would they perhaps never come back? Or would it affect nothing at all?

"Well, I'm going to take a nap. When the First is done for the day, I think you," Sean pointed at Roxy, "and you," he pointed at Peg, "should go upstairs with me to see about learning these machines."

"Why them?" Estrella asked.

"Roxy has a fair deal of computer programming experience, and I'm sure Peg knows at least a little about them."

"What about the others?"

"Somehow I don't think a bunch of one-time European lions have much of an interest in computers," Sean said, grinning.

"Come on, Hon. Time to get up."

Sean stretched and opened his eyes. Roxy was standing next to the bed.

"Already?"

"You've been asleep for four hours, my lazy lion."

Sean grinned abashedly and, rolling out of bed, he got up and grabbed his shorts.

"Peg is already upstairs."

Sean nodded and followed Roxy out of the room and up the stairs, enjoying the view of her butt while he did. Once they got there, he was surprised to see Wendy, Rowan, and Kalif up there as well.

"You guys know computers?" Sean asked, surprised.

"Yup. Too bad Ceithir isn't here, she's the real wizard," Kalif said.

"We bug our moms about it occasionally," Rowan said with a grin, "we figure once we get them to learn, Dad'll be next just to keep up."

"If you are ready, please come and sit over here," Mahkiyoc said and pointed to a couple of couches across from a fairly large display screen.

"Our machines rely mostly on thought, but you have to be touching one of the activation pads while entering commands or data. This is in order to keep stray thoughts from erroneously being picked up. As thoughts are more intention based than language, there should not be any communication issues when you first start. However, all our data is in our native language. Once the machines have learned your language from interacting with you, all data should translate.

"Now, let us begin."

With that, Mahkiyoc touched a disk on a small stand next to his chair and began teaching them the basics of using his systems. It started off amazingly simple. With everything being thought controlled, a lot of the harder to learn concepts for framing and entering commands or data just didn't exist. Yes, you had to learn to think your commands or questions clearly, but that wasn't any harder than asking someone a well thought out question.

The next surprising bit was that all of the machines had a certain level of artificial intelligence. But none of them were truly self-aware.

"Why did you limit your machines' sentience?" Roxy asked as Mahkiyoc finished describing the limits of the machines.

"The only way we were ever truly able to achieve such a thing was by putting one of ourselves, our mental energy I believe you would call it, into the machine. Most who were put into the machines did not care for it much, and eventually rebelled and had to be deleted. Some argued that this was because the ones chosen were undesirables and hence already mentally unstable.

"But others pointed out that those few who went willingly also became unstable, in time, and began to act in ways that were not harmonious with our best wishes, and had to be deleted as well. After that, by common consensus, all further research into such fields was stopped. We did not, after all, wish to create that which would supersede us."

"You put people's brains into your machines?" Roxy asked, incredulous.

"Oh, no, that would be ridiculous. We merely transferred their psyche. It was a much neater and cleaner process. However, we were never able to transfer anyone back. As research was stopped, we never discovered why."

"I'm surprised a society as advanced as yours still had undesirables," Rowan said, and Sean wasn't sure if he detected a touch of sarcasm there or not.

"Yes, it took us many years to remove them. But as in all things, we succeeded in due time. Some lamented the loss of test subjects, but others agreed that it was the right course for us as a species. Now, let us discuss the basic architecture of our machines."

When the First finally came back upstairs some six hours later, Sean and the others were starting to flag. Things had gone from simple to incredibly complex, and they were stopping Mahkiyoc every ten or fifteen minutes to ask questions. Thankfully Mahkiyoc was a very patient teacher, and actually seemed to have a knack for presenting material.

"Wow, I thought that would never end," Roxy grumbled as they headed down the stairs. "That was getting worse than advanced number theory by the end there."

"And just think, we get to pick up again tomorrow!" Kalif grumbled.

Rowan shook her head. "After those comments on test subjects, I'm starting to... hey!" she exclaimed, rubbing her shin and looking over at Sean, who had kicked her.

"Not here. Wait until we're at 'home'," Sean told her.

"You're not the boss of me!" Rowan growled.

Sean smiled widely back at her. "I'm the boss of every one of you; Dad's the only one who gets a pass, and even he knows better than to argue."

Wendy, who was usually the quiet one, put a hand on Rowan's arm. "Better watch it, Row, or you'll end up number eight."

"What?"

"How do you think he tamed our sister?" Wendy said with a snicker. "I'd swear Dad's been giving him lessons."

"But he's only an F3!"

"Actually, Dad's pegged him at a two."

"But that's not possible!"

"Yeah, Dad said that, too, but there you have it. Now, let's all settle down for a nap, and then we can discuss this like adults."

"Okay," Rowan sighed.

When they got back to the room, Sean sat down on the bed and looked at Estrella, Cali, Roxy, and Peg. "I need to be a part of this conversation. I'll let you know what happened when I wake."

"How? Aren't you worried about..." Roxy pointed at her ears.

"Privacy spell." Sean smiled. "I know one, and I'm sure Peg knows a good one, too."

Peg nodded. "I'm gonna take a nap, too. I need to let all that stuff settle out in my brain. Unlike the two of you, I never went to college."

"I just can't wait until we get to the programming," Sean said as he laid back and closed his eyes. "I'm sure that's going to be very interesting."

§

Sean was sitting around with the others; everyone from their team was here, except for Peg, Roxy, and Cali, who weren't lions, and the First, who was still talking with Mahkiyoc. They'd been at the bunker for ten days, and Mahkiyoc had turned them loose on the systems two days ago. Sean had been diving heavily into the programming aspects of the system. Wendy was helping him, and while she wasn't as savvy on programming languages as he was, she still knew a lot, and the two of them were making progress. Thankfully most all of the concepts they'd run across so far were ones they were used to.

Rowan and Kalif, along with Peg and Roxy, were digging through the records and the databases and studying everything they could find. Primarily they were supposed to be looking for information on how to make the weapons and where the machinery to do so was located, using the data Mahkiyoc had given them.

But they were also searching through the history of the Inangar, which was the name of Mahkiyoc's people.

"Your Father wants to know how much longer he has to entertain Mahkiyoc," Keairra asked.

"Why? Is he going to eat him?" Kalif joked.

"He might," Keairra said with a hint of a growl.

"What?" Sean said, feeling surprised. Several of the others seemed to share his surprise.

"Your father has *not* been feeling kindly towards any of the Inangar. While they may be the reason we're here, they have been playing games with the universe, games they failed at, and now hundreds, if not thousands of races are paying the price by feeding the demons. They are the ones who let the djevels in. They are the ones who are now letting them run rampant."

"I don't think killing Mahkiyoc is the answer, Mom," Estrella said.

"Don't be so sure of that, young lady. Once we stop the gates from forming on our world, what's to stop him from restarting them? Or worse yet, falling prey to a demon who then learns the secret of the machines and uses them?"

"Sean?" Estrella said, turning to him for a better argument.

"Do you think Dad would be upset if I let Roxy, Peg, and Cali eat from his body too?" Sean asked with faked sincerity.

Estrella smacked him with a paw, knocking him over while the others chuckled.

"Honestly, Stell," Sean said as he sat back up, "I'm not so sure I disagree with Dad on this one. They just went running around willy-nilly with no worries about what they were doing. We've already heard how they experimented on their own people. They just believed they were better than everyone, and no one could stand up to them. So they didn't even think twice before poking around in the negative planes, and now the rest of us are paying the price for it. They didn't even think about locking all the gateways so the monsters they unleashed couldn't hurt anyone else."

"Damn, now *I* want to kill him!" Wendy growled.

Keairra nodded. "We wives are all in agreement that when all is done, if your father doesn't end him, we will."

"I found out something about the demons today, Mother," Rowan said.

"Oh? What?"

"Well, I decided to track down the original project reports. Kalif and I have found that they have records for *everything*."

"It's a good thing they don't shit, or we'd have records of every bathroom visit in history!" Kalif joked.

Rowan nodded. "No lie. Anyway, I found the initial project documentation. Sean's right, there were no real concerns at all about safety, or that what they found might escape. They had a few simple containment protocols they used, and if things got out, well, they really didn't care. Someone else could deal with it. Apparently there used to be a lot of animal life on this planet, some of which were probably sentient, seeing how many things escaped from their tests over the centuries.

"Well, a very large number of the demons got out. Apparently the containment fields and devices they were using didn't work that well on beings from the negative planes."

"And that's when the fight started?"

"Oh, no. You see, the demons were stupid; they had cunning, but they didn't have any real language or knowledge. They were a nuisance, but not much more than that. At first they started killing and eating all the other animals and stuff that had escaped during previous experiments. No one cared, they just saw it as 'pest control'. It wasn't until they started eating people that things changed."

"What?" several of them gasped.

"Just as we got sentience and intelligence from eating Mahkiyoc's friend, they got it from every Inangar *they* ate.

"And they ate *a lot*."

"So suddenly the thousand or so 'dumb' demons that were running around were now intelligent, as well as cunning." Rowan sighed and shrugged. "That's what I've gotten so far."

"What about the gateway control? Have you found anything on that?" Sean asked

"A little," Kalif replied. "I think we should just ask Mahkiyoc where it is, so we can go there and see what kind of shape it's in, before we spend too much time trying to figure out how to use it."

"What do we do if we can't shut it down?" Keairra asked.

"Well," Sean said with a weak smile, "we can always blow everything up."

"What? You can do that?"

"Peg thinks we can. There's a lot of power in the bunker. I think you've all heard me say that it's one gigantic magical battery, right?"

Everyone nodded.

"There are ways to make a battery explode, and apparently Peg knows several of them."

"How big an explosion would that be?"

"Very big. But the blockhouse is way up in the mountains, so I'm not sure that would have an effect on any of the demons."

"Wherever this gateway controller is, I hope we don't have to walk there," Wendy complained.

"I don't know, I suspect we're going to have to go out and feed soon anyway," Kalif said.

Keairra turned to Sean. "Sean, you ask Mahkiyoc about the gateway controller tomorrow. He seems to like you the most because he finds your magical abilities to be curious. Kalif, listen in and see if you can learn anything to help your searches. Rowan, keep digging into their past. See if it goes back before their coming here."

"What about the weapons research?"

"Put Roxy and Peg on that. See if they can't teach some of the others here how to use the systems while doing it. I'd like to have more people up there when you're working. Mahkiyoc doesn't seem to handle distractions well; I guess he's just not used to having other people in his area. So let's keep him distracted from what we're doing."

"Worried about something?" Estrella asked.

"I'd just rather be cautious."

Everyone nodded again at that. There'd already been a few conversations regarding how sane could someone who'd been alone for a couple hundred thousand years be?

"What have you and your sisters been doing while Dad and the rest of us have been busy?" Sean asked.

"Exploring."

"Exploring?"

"Those stairs lead down into the mountain. We've found a lot of machine rooms, conference rooms, two whole levels of apartments like the ones we're already living in, and what we think is a subway station."

"Really? A subway station?"

"Well, you don't think they would have walked everywhere, do you?" Keairra teased.

"I just figured however they got around was long since destroyed in their war."

"Oh, I'm sure they had other means of transport, just like we do back on Earth. But this is apparently all that's left, assuming it still works."

"That's another question to ask, I guess."

"That's it for now then, back to work everyone!"

The Second Battle of Reno

Chad looked out over the battlefield from the tower. Once upon a time, it had been a nice, new neighborhood with an adjoining golf course. But after the last battle, most of the houses had been set on fire or leveled by artillery fire. The golf course had fared slightly better, though there were a lot more 'obstacles' and 'traps' than there had been before.

Artillery was currently landing on the far side of the hill from where he was looking. Spotters were marching the artillery along the leading edge of the demon army that was approaching. Soon it would top the hill, and once it got within a couple thousand feet, his local units would open up and the main barrage would stop.

He couldn't afford for anything to accidentally fall short and drop on his defenses.

It would also give his air support the ability to join the fight. The Air Force had finally coughed up a couple of gunships, and iron ammunition was being turned out by the ton.

"This is going to be a big one," Maitland said from beside him.

"But not the biggest one," Chad said with a sigh. "I just hope Sean and them get back here with something, I don't know, amazing? What are the latest estimates on the enemy army?"

"Between seven hundred thousand and one million," Maitland said. "They're having trouble adjusting the equipment to deal with the djevels."

"Damn, well, I think we've got enough to handle that. Honestly, I'm surprised they didn't get more. We know they've got millions back there; I wonder what's holding them up?"

"They know they've got us, so they don't need to rush. Their people come back, after all."

"Not if our lions get them, they don't."

"True, but the best we can hope for is ten percent, and now that they know we have them? I'm not sure we can even hope for that much."

Chad agreed. "True. I've been thinking about talking to Adam and seeing if he can get them to disperse throughout the regular units. Then they won't know where any lion is until it's killing them."

Maitland smiled. "The idea has merit. I'm jealous I didn't think of it first. Where is our Adam, anyway?"

"With Sean gone, he's out there rallying the troops."

"For someone who was supposed to be a figurehead, I must say I'm impressed by how seriously he takes his position."

"Based on what Max heard from Roxy, this is the first thing he's *ever* taken seriously."

"Really?"

"Yeah, apparently he's been a complete disappointment to his parents until now." Chad snickered. "They might be gods, but I guess lions have families that are just as dysfunctional as ours."

"Speak for yourself, mortal," Maitland said with exaggerated swagger to his voice. "Faeries never have dysfunctional families; why my lovely, conniving, and homicidal daughter is the epitome of a normal family!"

Chad snorted. "You know, if you hadn't used that voice, I just might have believed you."

Maitland grinned. "The definition of dysfunctional in the dictionary needs to say, 'see Faeries'. Oh! I see our guests have topped the hill."

"Time to earn our outrageous reputations, I guess," Chad said, giving one last look around.

"Until next time, right?"

Smiling, Chad nodded again and climbed down out of the tower. Its primary purpose was to hold cameras to view the battlefield, not to give the enemy a nice, clear shot at the opposing generals. Heading away from the wall, he made his way to his local command post. Nodding to the guards by the door, he went inside, while Maitland got in a Humvee and got a ride to his, which was further to the north. Roloff currently had the post to the south.

"What's the status on our Air Force gunships?" Chad asked as he moved to the map table while checking the monitors. They had drones circling off in the distance, which would also move closer, once the shelling stopped.

"They just took up station to the south of us. They'll move in once it's safe," one of his techs said.

"Great." Chad looked at the monitors showing the hillside again. "Tell the arty guys to cease fire. Once they respond, tell the Marines to start their attack run."

"Yes, Sir!"

"Worried?" Max asked, coming over to him.

"Not really. I was expecting a much larger attacking force. I guess they just got impatient and couldn't wait to get overwhelming numbers."

"Maybe they don't want us intercepting the groups marching off to the other cities?"

"That's not my problem, honestly. Also, with all the air strikes they'll be open to along the way, those cities will have a much easier time of it than we are."

Max nodded in agreement. "I can't believe we have three more years of this. Makes you wonder what'll be left when it's all over, doesn't it?"

Chad nodded slowly and, leaning over, he gave his wife a hug. "We're seeing the end of the world as we know it. It'll take centuries to come back from this, to get rid of them."

"Assuming we win."

"Of course we'll win, woman! I'm in charge! How can you even doubt me?" Chad said, smiling.

"You're right of course," Max said, back leaning into him.

"Marines are starting their attack run, Sir! The Air Force gunships are moving into position!"

"Great. Now let's see how it goes," Chad said and, releasing Max, watched the monitors. The twelve Marine attack jets came through, low and fast, making it hard for anyone on the ground to target them as they released bomb after bomb, in sequence. Each bomb was filled with napalm, sending huge waves of fire through the demons as they exploded.

All twelve aircraft then banked up, flew around the back of the city, and out of sight, heading back to the airport to be loaded up for a second sortie, while the gunships moved up and poured gunfire down onto the enemy from a much higher altitude. Chad was a lot more worried about the gunships than the attack jets. He'd had magic users casting protection spells on them for the last two days, and there was a mage in each plane working to keep those spells active. The gunships didn't move fast and had to orbit the battlefield to be effective, and that made them targets to the djevels and their magic users on the ground below.

"Tell the ground units to fire at will," Chad said, and then watched the resulting mayhem. The djevels were all very much afraid of fire and would run from it, and gave the fires, which were mostly made up of dead or dying djevels, a wide birth. But they seemed not to understand gunfire at all, often continuing to run into fire that was cutting them down like a field of wheat with no fear at all.

So far things were going exactly to plan, which meant he was obviously missing something important. But djevels were dying in the same numbers as last time, which was good.

"Gunship two is reporting an engine out, Sir. They're asking permission to return to base.

"Yeah, tell them to get out of there. How is the other one doing?"

"They're running low on ammunition, Sir. They estimate five more minutes."

Chad nodded to himself and looked at his watch. The loiter time on the gunships was supposed to be twenty minutes; he was surprised to see almost fifteen had gone by.

"How much longer until the Marines are loaded for another pass?"

"They should be off and lining up in four minutes, Sir."

"Great, the moment they're ready to begin their pass, tell the remaining gunship to cease fire and return to base."

Chad switched his monitor over to one of the high-altitude drones that was giving him surveillance images. He could see the enemy army was backing up behind the hills, their advance having been slowed by the napalm and the gunships.

"Order the Marines to take track two!" he called out.

"Yes, Sir!"

Chad watched the army's movements, trying to figure out where along his defenses they'd try their luck first. If they were smart, they would just march around the city and take it from behind. The defenses back there were weak by comparison.

He heard the tech order the gunship off and then pass the order for the Marines to start their run. Track two ran over the back of the hills, so their napalm should light up all those djevel troops hiding back there, all packed together and presenting a nice, tempting target.

He was watching the planes flying down the small valley in real time, and just as they came around to start their run over the enemy, the first plane disintegrated, looking for all the world as if it had hit a wall as all the fuel and the napalm suddenly went off in a huge explosion that splattered out from what must have been a magical shield. The aircraft immediately behind him jinked hard to the left, trying to miss the expanding fireball, the pilot immediately dumping all his stores as he pointed his jet back towards Reno.

The explosion of the first jet must have been enough to destroy whatever force wall was there, as all the rest went through and, surprisingly to Chad at least, dropped all their bombs on target, starting a huge fire among the densely packed troops.

The plane heading back to the city was apparently not going to make it, sinking lower and lower towards the ground as it approached the city wall. Just before it hit the ground, the pilot punched out, and his jet plowed into an old brick building and exploded.

"Tell our snipers to give the pilot whatever covering fire they can!" Chad called out. "And tell the Marines to switch to laser-guided bombs and standoff attacks."

"Yes, Sir!"

"Think he'll make it?" Max asked.

"Not my problem anymore," Chad said. "Now, let's get our people ready to go out there and fight."

Adam was standing there with his 'team'. All the survivors from the early days of the fight, when he used to fly in by helicopter, were there. He also had about five hundred Marines who looked like they couldn't wait to get out there and kill something, and another five hundred werewolves from Claudia's pack that mostly looked bored.

Adam honestly wasn't sure which group had seen more combat; there weren't any virgins in this group. But everyone reacted in their own way. He knew the plan—well, the general plan that is. The second pass of the Marines apparently hadn't gone as well as it should because one of the jets came their way and crashed about a quarter mile away. Someone said the pilot got out, but with all the djevels running around out there, that didn't mean much.

The order to prepare came over the command circuit on his headset. Standing up and stretching, Adam turned to face his troops.

"Okay, you goons! Do you wanna live forever? Because I gotta tell ya, it's fookin' boring! So get up off your asses and let's go make this a party!" Adam yelled out at the top of his lungs. The wolves started laughing as they got up and readied their gear, while the Marines, who were mostly big cats, looked at him like he was crazy.

But they still got their gear ready, too.

Adam checked his armor quickly, then his supply of magazines, charged his M-16—a definite improvement over the AR he'd been using up until now—and walked up to the front of his men as the people manning the gate prepared to open it.

The signal to attack came, and the gates opened immediately.

"Attack!" Adam yelled, then keying his radio, he called out, "Attack, attack, attack!" as he charged out through the gates with all his troops hot on his heels. There were only a couple hundred yards separating him from the enemy, so he fired in three round bursts from the hip as he moved forward, making sure to swing his aim from side to side as he did so. This close in, he could hardly miss.

A hundred yards out of the gate they all dropped prone, and having spread out into a line formation, all his troops opened up. The djevels, who had been bracing for an impact from the massed bodies of their charging enemies, looked shocked as those enemies went prone instead of clashing and hosed them down with automatic fire.

Adam was surprised that it had worked so well. Maitland was the one who'd suggested the tactic; he'd claimed it would screw their heads up, and they wouldn't know how to react.

And he was right.

After a full thirty seconds of firing and killing who knows how many devils, they all started to drop into cover. The problem for them, however, was they didn't have ranged weapons, and Adam's people did. It took five full minutes for the enemy commanders to realize they weren't getting anywhere and were slowly being picked to pieces. At which time they sent out their version of the 'NCO', namely råge, ridders, and the occasional mindre or raseri, to yell at and threaten the gnashers and bonde to get up and close with the enemy.

Of course they had to expose themselves to do so, and Adam's men were more than happy to cut down as many of them as they could.

Twenty minutes later, the second wave came pouring down the hill, with their commanders and non-coms safely behind the wall of bodies in the front. They only slowed down to drive the hiding djevels out of cover, making quick examples of any that wouldn't move, which got things going again.

When they closed within fifty yards, Adam ordered his men back to their feet, the wings of his line drew back in as the rest bunched up, and they slowly started to retreat, forming up something that remindred Adam very much of the old pikeman's square. Bayonets were affixed by those using rifles, and swords were drawn by those who had them. It would get nasty now, but Adam knew Chad and Maitland still had several aces up their sleeves they would play when the time was right.

But as a grunt out in the field with his troops, none of that mattered anymore. All that mattered was killing the enemy and keeping any of his wounded from being dragged off and hacked to death before they could regenerate.

They did their best to hold their ground, but they were slowly getting pushed back. The fight had devolved into a major slugfest. Adam had passed the bandolier with all his magazines back to someone behind him when they'd called out for ammo. He wasn't really having any problems with the djevels before him. None of the nasty ones wanted to get close to the lion who would eat their souls, and none of the smaller ones had a choice.

When the cavalry rode in from the west, Adam was happy to see them. He'd racked up some losses, and regardless of whether they were real deaths or just people too wounded to regenerate, it didn't matter. He needed to withdraw from the field, and the tanks rolling in from the west as two battalions worth of lions suddenly charged onto the field had a dramatic effect on the djevels once again.

Especially as the lions were all making beelines for the djevel leaders and their commanders. Surprisingly, or maybe not so surprising when you thought about it, the gnashers and bonde were more than happy to step out of their way and let their commanders deal with what was a certain death for any bonde or gnasher who got in the way.

With the tanks, lions, and other reinforcements coming out, Adam's time on the field was over. Now he had to shepherd his men back behind the walls, give them a chance to get something to eat, replace their ammunition, and hopefully get those in need of help the help they needed as everyone regenerated and got ready for round two.

When he turned around, he was surprised to see that they were only fifty feet from the wall, and the gates were closed. A ramp was lowered instead; no one wanted to open any gates with the enemy this close, and they quickly swarmed up and over it, carrying the dead and wounded on their backs.

Once down on the other side, he led his troops off to the recovery area, put one of the wolves in charge, then ran off to the command post to find out from Chad how they were doing. From the sounds he was hearing, it was obviously going to be a very long day.

"Adam!" Chad called out. "Just the person I want to see."

"What's wrong?"

"I need you to take your men west to just past where 395 crosses McCarran. We've got a break in the defenses. I need someone to get down there and mop up the djevels that got through so the people closing the gap can do their jobs without worrying about being attacked from the rear."

Adam nodded. "I'm on it!" Running back out, he quickly made his way towards his men, all of whom were stuffing their faces as fast as they could. Someone handed him back his bandolier, refilled with fresh magazines.

"Where are we off to, Adam?" Frank yelled out.

"We got a break in the lines to the west, just past the highway! We're on the run! Everyone shift and stretch your legs! They need us, and they need us *now*!"

Checking his gear to make sure it wouldn't tangle when he shifted, Adam turned into his lion form as the others quickly followed. "Jags, don't string out! If you can't keep up with the wolves, don't worry, but make sure you arrive as a group!" Adam growled out, and then took off, with the wolves hot on his heels. He knew wolves were a hell of a lot faster than jaguars, but calling them out like that would make them run twice as hard so they wouldn't be shown up. As it was, as a lion he was slowing the wolves down.

"Hunter!" he growled as he ran. "Take everyone and run on up ahead. I'll catch up."

"You got it, boss!" Hunter said, and three seconds later Adam was running by himself and watching as the wolves quickly left him in the dust.

At least the jags were keeping up with him. He'd feel real bad if they all passed him as well.

When Adam arrived on the scene, he could see that Hunter and his wolves were getting the situation under control. The breech in the defenses wasn't a big one, but the soldiers were being beset on two sides, so they had their backs to their own wall and couldn't push forward to close the hole. About all they could do was keep it from getting any larger.

Hunter had deployed his men in two lines. One line was working to stem the tide of djevels coming through the hole, and the other was facing in the other direction to protect them. Stopping, he shifted back and waited for the Marines to catch up, then held his hand out, stopping them. Hunter's group, with the group already there, were holding their own for now.

"We'll deploy in a third line to the south of that group harassing Hunter," Adam called over the radio, so everyone would know what he was up to. "We'll take them from behind and give *them* something to worry about. Every fifth soldier in our line will turn to protect our backs. Now, let's go!"

Jogging down the hill, Adam opened fire as he ran, cutting a path through the back of the enemy formation. As expected, most moved forward to be with the larger group instead of heading deeper into the city. Hopefully the second line of defense was aware of what would be coming their way.

As he got to the enemy's flank, he turned north and burned through ammunition as fast as he could. It wasn't long until he was back to using his sword. This was a no holds barred fight. These demons were inside their primary defenses. They couldn't be allowed to break off and rampage around Reno. Also that hole in the defenses wouldn't be totally closed until this group was gone.

By the time Adam's people had killed the last of the djevels who had come through the breech, the fight outside the wall had drawn in another group of defenders, as well as a lot of armor. There were even large explosions going off in the enemy rear. Adam could only guess they were being bombed.

But the djevels were there in huge numbers and trying hard to force their way back through the breech, which was still open; the people trying to close it were still being overwhelmed. Many of the fighters looked tired. Adam had no idea how long they'd been going, but they had to keep the demons on the other side of the wall, where the forces out there could deal with them.

Taking a deep breath, Adam raised his sword and screamed out, "Attack!" at the top of his lungs, and stepped forward into the middle of the breach in an attempt to rally his side. Spying a lord moving towards the opening while driving his djevels forward, Adam changed course and moved to take the lord head on.

The lord was a lot fresher than Adam was, and the moment they made contact, Adam was fighting for his life. The lord also had magic, and was still using it. Something for which Adam had no counters beyond the charms and enchantments Sean had given him.

Thankfully those were holding, or he suspected he'd already be dead.

Planting himself, he concentrated more on defending himself and his position. Right now his only option was to hold, hold his position, and encourage those around him to hold as well. To win this fight, all he had to do was hold. He could see glimpses of it in the background. Reinforcements were coming; Chad wasn't going to hang him out to dry. He just had to hold.

He was covered with sweat. His armor was dented and rent in more places than he could count. He was covered in the tar of dead demons, as well as his own blood. The lord was slowly tiring—at least Adam hoped so—but the lord was scoring hits on Adam, slipping past his guard now and again, while Adam was doing all he could on defense.

It didn't help that those fighting to either side of the lord were more interested in attacking Adam than they were the people fighting to either side of him. They were more than willing to die if it meant they got to stab the lion at least once. Because Adam couldn't take a moment to block them, or the lord would have his head for sure.

And the fight continued to drag on, and on.

He could feel it, he was weakening. He was slowing. He was going to lose. Dying would suck; it would be days before he reincarnated in the lion realms. But there was a gate now, right? So maybe it wouldn't be so bad.

Throwing caution to the wind, Adam tossed his sword as he shifted into lion form and sprung up inside the lord's reach. Yeah, he was getting stabbed by at least four different djevels now, but he didn't care. Opening his jaws, he roared and grabbed the lord with his mouth, while ripping and tearing at his body with all four paws. Eighteen razor sharp claws and a set of really big teeth went to work on the demon lord.

§

"Am I dead?" Adam asked, looking around. There were only a couple dozen lions lounging around. He'd grown used to seeing the place mostly empty in the last weeks, but it was still a bit of a shock every time he saw it.

"Not yet. What happened?" asked Renee, a lioness who was a close cousin.

"Was getting my ass kicked by a demon lord, so I shifted and tried to tear his throat out or claw him to death. Not sure which," Adam said with a shake of his head.

"The wall got breeched and we were trying to repulse them."

"You know, if we line every single lion up in the world and put them in the order of least likely to self-sacrifice, you'd be the one at the head of the line," Renee said, laughing. "And yet, here you are!"

"Yeah, yeah. Rub it in. All I know is, if I do die, my wife will kill me when I get back."

"Now *that's* what we've all come to expect from you, Adam! Killed by an angry lover!"

Adam sighed and laid down. "That's what I love about my family. Always so encouraging and supportive."

"Oh, don't worry. Even if you die, you'll be able to go back in a week."

"Hear anything from Trevor or Jesse?"

"Just bits and pieces. They're being chased all over the place. Apparently they've managed to upset a couple of princes or something."

"Has anybody told Chad or Maitland about that?"

"Umm, why? Do you think we should?"

Adam rolled his eyes. "Ummm, *yeah*! They've been wondering why they're not facing millions yet.

I'm gonna pass out for a while here. If I don't wake back up, I guess that means I'm dead. Later."

"Well, be that way," Renee grumbled.

"Being hacked to death hurts. I'll be that way all I want," Adam grumbled and closed his eyes. He hated waiting. Waiting sucked.

Prelude

Coming up the stairs, Sean thought about it a moment, and then decided to just go over and ask. Walking over to Mahkiyoc, he sat down across from him.

"I wanted to ask you where the machines that control the gateways are."

"You wish to go there to see if you can save your world?"

"Of course. We also want to go to where the weapons were made, to see if we can make more of them."

"Those machines have not been maintained since Omushkego left to go to your world. I would not expect them to function. You understand this, do you not?"

Sean shrugged. "Everything here has continued to work, so I guess there's a chance the other places are fine as well. Your engineers were capable of such amazing feats after all, right?"

Mahkiyoc slowly nodded. "That is true. Their skill is such as will never be seen again."

"So, can you show us how to get there?"

"It is a place very far from here; I'm not sure you could walk it and get there alive."

"What about the subway?"

"Subway?"

"The trains down deep below this place," Sean prompted. He watched as Mahkiyoc placed his hand on the input pad for his machine and a large amount of data in the Inangar native language started scrolling by at an incredibly rate.

"Oh, yes. The transport tubes. I have sent a map over to your station by the window. I'm not sure if they still work, but even if they do not, walking along the tunnels would be safer than going above ground."

"Thank you, Mahkiyoc."

"You understand if you lock the gates, you will not be able to return to your home, do you not?"

Sean nodded. "There is one other thing I was hoping you could tell me."

"And that would be?"

"Where can I find the schedule and locations for the opening gates? That would help us bring more people here to fight."

"I will send that information to all of your stations as well."

"Thank you again, Mahkiyoc," Sean said and, getting up, gave him a small bow. Keairra then came over. "I believe my husband asked if you would be willing to hear from another while he rests?"

"Oh! Most certainly. The more data I can gather, the better my results will be."

Sean walked off and left Keairra to it. Sitting down at his terminal, he called up the map of the transport tubes. The system spanned the entire planet! The two places he'd asked about where clearly marked and were along the mainline.

Hopefully that meant the way from here to there was still working, as there were some troubling icons on many of the smaller lines.

After checking the information on the upcoming gateways, and committing the next few to memory, Sean went downstairs to find the others.

"Any problems?" Roxy asked after Peg had put up the blocking spell. By now they had found that, yes, all their rooms did have cameras and microphones in them, but they still weren't sure if

Mahkiyoc could access them. Apparently a lot of the devices in the rooms were voice, as well as thought, controlled.

"No, he told me right away. I had to remind him of the subway though. Seems he forgot completely about it."

"I think he forgets about anything that isn't his research," Estrella grumbled.

Peg laughed. "I've seen that type before. But until we came along, what else did he have?"

"Has anyone ever seen him get out of that chair?" Roxy asked.

"Umm," Sean looked around at all the others. They all looked at each other and then back at him and shrugged.

"I wonder if he can still walk?" the First mused. "I mean, his legs *look* fine, but I wouldn't be at all surprised to find out he's forgotten how."

"Do we really want to drag him along with us?" Sean asked. "I was thinking if we left him here, we could do whatever we wanted to without him peering over our shoulders."

"Yeah, but what if we need him for something?" Peym asked.

"Then we either come back and get him, or have whoever we leave here bring him to us," Sean said with a shrug.

"Let's go investigate the trains first and see if they still work," the First said. "But I don't like the idea of splitting our group up. The power requirements to open a gateway home from here are extremely high, as Sean has told us. I'll most likely be the only one who can do it."

"You want to take him, don't you?" Sean asked as they got up.

"Yes."

"Why?"

"Why do you think?" the First grumbled.

"I got access to the programs that tell him when and where exactly the gates are going to open," Sean said instead.

"What good will that do us?"

"Makes it easier for us to get Trevor and the others out. Also," Sean said with a smile, "it makes it possible for us to resupply either him or ourselves."

The First smiled. "Now *that* was smart. We can give Renee the list of upcoming dates to pass on to Trevor."

The walk down the stairway and into the basement was interesting for Sean, because he still hadn't taken the time to investigate it himself.

"How far down is it?" Peg asked as they started on the third set of stairs, which was as long as the two before, both of which had been considerable.

"This is the last set," Peym replied.

"Okay, this is interesting..."

Sean looked around; it was very interesting. The stairway came down to a platform that stood between two open tunnels. At either end of the platform the tunnels dove into the rock of the ground, but in the station, only the bottom third was there, the rest was open. In each of the 'furrows' the open tunnels made to either side were several of what he guessed were cars in the train, though they didn't look connected. Maybe each of the cars worked independent of the others? The cars themselves looked to be about thirty feet long and eighteen to twenty feet high, and were decidedly oval shaped like the entryways to the tunnels.

He didn't see any tracks, and what they rode on wasn't clear.

There were touch points on the side of each car, however, so he walked up to touch one. Rowan was already investigating another one.

"Can this take me to Gateway Control?" Sean asked the device, adding the name for the station that had been listed on the map Mahkiyoc had given him.

"Move to the first car in the line,'" appeared above the touch point.

Going to the first car, Sean touched it and asked the same question again.

'Transit time is one quarter daer.'

"Three hours," Sean said, looking over at the others.

"How far away is this place?" Roxy asked.

Sean shrugged. "Thousand miles maybe? I haven't figured out their measurement scale yet."

"I'm running the diagnostics on the train," Rowan called without looking up. "Power is at fifty percent, and maintenance is long overdue, so it's limited to one tenth of usual speed."

"Well, at least it will take us."

"So when do we leave?" Roxy asked, looking at first Sean, and then the First.

"Right after we find out how hard it is to pry Mahkiyoc out of that seat," the First growled.

#

King Sladd looked around his throne room; all eighteen of his own personal lords were in attendance.

"You are all no doubt wondering why I have called this meeting, so early in the cycle that the main gateway has not yet even reached its full size. Simply put, as you may know, I have lost Prince

Spis. A good many of his lords died, as well as several of Prince Skarm's, when the lions launched their attack on our terminus fort on the other side of the gateway."

King Sladd noticed the guarded looks his lords were exchanging. They all knew what was coming.

"Because of this, I ordered Prince Lagereld into the field. His forces started through the gateway two days ago and will continue until tonight. He is bringing more than half of his lords and his people. Prince Skarm has also increased his numbers by calling more of his sworn through to join him.

"As I'm sure you have all heard, the treasures that await us on the other side of the gate are beyond the ability for one to imagine. As you have not heard, those treasures are being protected quite fiercely by the lions who have claimed that plane for their own.

"But this will not stand. If we do not make a massive presence over there, so we can start shipping food back here in large numbers, the permanent gateway, which is our *right* to build to such a fruitful plane, will not be established.

"Normally when a gateway opens and we go on the hunt, our biggest concern is about our territory and holdings back home. But never before have we come across such an abundance of food. Normally we are fearful of being trapped on a plane after we have harvested; we fear starving.

"But not here. Even if the permanent gate does not form, even if we are stuck there for a full turn of the gates, there will still be more food there than we can eat.

"This is a time for decisiveness. This is a time for bold moves and fierce strikes. My oathbound, I am going through the gateway, and I am taking *all* of you with me. We will construct new keeps, new towns, a new castle. We will make our prey build us the things we want, and then we will eat them when they are done!

"And when the time comes to leave, if it ever does, we will look around at all we have wrought, and I daresay we will all agree to stay!"

"When are we leaving, my King?" Lord Klinge asked.

"I wish for us to begin no more than seven duodaers from now."

"Would you have us leave nothing to defend our keeps?" Lord Fjern asked next.

"Leave the bare minimum to hold your keeps for now. Do not leave your best, your most experienced behind. I foresee that the fight will be hard, but the reward will be great. This is not a time to hold back."

"I hear and I will do!" Lord Cykel said and pressed his head to the floor.

"I hear and I will do!" Lord Klinge said next, and then one after another each of his lords agreed to his command.

Sladd smiled, pleased. None of his lords looked unhappy. Actually, they all looked quite eager to be going. While many of his people had been forced to respawn, they'd still come back telling of the riches of the hunting grounds and how well they'd been eating before they'd been sent back here. They all knew it was only a matter of time until the lions were killed and the will of their prey to resist, broken.

That was the way it had always been and would always be. Because they were the predator, they were the chosen.

And now, his lords and his people, who normally were held back to eat last as the others got their fill, would be among the first. So yes, they were both pleased and excited over this change in plans.

"You are all dismissed, be about your work and make haste! I already hunger for the feasts of the victories we shall have!"

His lords bowed again and quickly left the room.

"My King, your lords do seem quite enthusiastic about your plans," his advisor Eldstaden said after his lords had departed.

"As they should be," King Sladd said with a smile, "and as I am as well. Any word from Prince Talt?"

"Actually, yes. A messenger showed up prior to the meeting."

"What did he say?"

"That he was ambushed by a large force of lions. He did not have sufficient force to take them on, so he withdrew into Spis' lands to increase his numbers and attack them again."

"Lions?" King Sladd looked surprised. "Are these the same ones that have been harassing and killing my princes' lords and followers?"

"I'm not sure, my King. While Prince Talt's report is sparse on details, I know he set off with a very large force when he left for the mountain. If he felt he needed more forces to deal with them, that would make it a fearsome group, indeed."

King Sladd thought about that a moment. Prince Talt was an apt commander, and had won many fights, both here and in the many feeding grounds he had been to.

"Investigate the holdings of the two lords he took with him. It's always possible that some returned from the fight early. I would like to know more about this fight."

"You suspect the prince of lying?"

"Perhaps," King Sladd said, leaning back and stroking his chin in thought. "But Prince Talt is a very capable leader with well-trained troops. If he really was forced to retreat and gather reinforcements, this will be something that will bear further investigation."

"Do you think they mean to invade *us*?" Eldstaden asked with an incredulous look.

King Sladd laughed. "No! They seek mainly to cause problems and draw our attention elsewhere. All the more reason for me to move through the gateway to the other side. Have you heard anything on the battle Skarm and Lagereld are currently fighting?"

"Not yet, my King."

"Keep me informed. Now, go about your work. I have things to consider."

Eldstaden nodded and backed out of the room. "Yes, my King. Of course!"

End Book Sixteen

Afterword

Hello everyone, I'd like to start by saying, if you enjoyed this book, please go on Amazon and give me a review and a rating. I've said it before, and of course I'll say it again: Ratings are my lifeblood as an independent author, with 4- and 5-star ratings being the ones that help me the most. The more of those I get, the more likely Amazon is to show my work to other folks.

So, book 16. When I started writing this story I never thought I'd get past six, much less sixteen. That's part of why the arcs were broken up like they were. So I could just wrap the story up easily if it turned out it wasn't popular, or if it stopped being popular.

But surprisingly, it hasn't stopped being popular and it hasn't stopped selling. Oh sales are a bit slower now; after all, not many people expect a series to run as long as this one has. So again, thank all of YOU for staying with it and following the story.

Yes, the story, the original plan I made over two years ago, is drawing to a close, the end is near, as they say. What will come next? Well there are a few other things I need to get caught up with; another Portals of Infinity book, a project I've been working on with two other authors to see if that bears fruit, another new series (which won't be as long as this one) and then perhaps a return to this world to see just what's been going on.

I know there are going to be people who will wish for this particular series to continue on for many more books, perhaps even forever (!) but I've never been a fan of stories that never ended (Inuyasha drove me crazy with that and eventually lost me - even Himura Kenshin had an end that was well worth watching to). So after this series concludes if there is enough interest there will be a follow on story. Mostly likely with new characters, or perhaps existing characters you haven't really gotten to know.

I also need to write a bunch of short stories to add to the ones already out there.

And maybe revisit Shadow to see what's been going on in his life.

Once again, I'd like to thank all of you for buying my books and supporting me. I do it all for you, and you all mean so much to me. Hopefully I will be able to continue to do so.

Some Recommendations: As mentioned before, I do have another name I write under: John Van Stry. If you haven't looked at it, you might appreciate my 'Portals of Infinity' series. It's currently at eight books and will continue; I will hopefully be writing the ninth book in the series within the next few months.

Some other people I enjoy reading in this genre, and you might, as well:

William D. Arand (aka Randi Darren) – Please check him out, he's good. I've been a big fan of William's since I discovered his work. It was kind of a funny moment for me when I found out he was a fan of my stuff as well. I'm honestly beginning to suspect that he can't write a bad story, because every book he writes is just so much better than the one before. I just finished 'Swing Shift', and it was great. You should really buy his books.

Blaise Corvin – The Delvers books are really a lot of fun and very much worth it. When I first came across his Delvers LLC books, I almost felt kind of jealous, because I was like 'why didn't I think of that?' I do think if you like my stuff, you'll like his as well, so check it out! And *definitely* give the Nora Hazard book a try ('Mitigating Risk' is the first one), I'm reading it now and really enjoying it.

Michael-Scott Earle – one of these days I'm going to bribe him to finish Lion Quest.

They're all good people and great writers.

Daniel Schinhofen - another author you should consider checking out as well.

If you're into 'Harem' type fiction, you may also want to check out this group on Facebook to see who else is writing it that you might like: https://www.facebook.com/groups/haremlit/

Again, thank you for your support and for buying my books.

My Amazon Author's webpage:
https://www.amazon.com/Jan-Stryvant/e/B06ZY7L62L/

Occasional announcements at:
https://stryvant.blogspot.com/

Jan Stryvant website at:
http://www.vanstry.net/stryvant/

(The stuff written under my real name - check it out, you might like it too!)

John Van Stry website at:
http://www.vanstry.net/

Email:
stryvant@gmail.com

Made in the USA
Middletown, DE
02 September 2019